Veridical Dreams Vol. I

ISBN: 978-0-9912039-9-4

 BEAT to a PULP
PO Box 173
Freeville, New York 13068
USA
Email: btapzine@beattoapulp.com
Visit us at www.beattoapulp.com

Based on the dream journals of KYLE J. KNAPP

A portion of the proceeds will go to higher education.

CONTENTS

For Meta, Bob, and Kayla

K J K

INTRODUCTION

I'm running through a dense forest—fast. My middle-aged body strong as I soar over fallen limbs and push aside branches. I hurtle over a mound of dirt and shrubbery, and crouch down at the edge of a vast, open field as arrows begin dropping all around me. I see a castle—my destination—in the distance. Off to the right of it is a small embankment and a familiar figure motioning for me to join him. He shoots a slew of arrows for cover and I make the run while cannon fire tears up the earth near me. With my last surge of energy, I leap wildly, landing next to my nephew who'd been providing protection.

"Glad you could make it, Uncle David," he says with a grin.

I'm gasping for air but manage, "Wouldn't miss this adventure for the world, Kyle."

Together we travel on to the base of the fortress. I shudder at the sheer size of the wall that stretches high into the sky above us. I look at Kyle, his muscles are corded, flexing for the challenge of the climb. He's ready to tackle it head on.

This recurring dream has a habit of varying in interpretation. At first it represented my concern with getting Kyle's work published, in doing it right, to perfection, trying to avoid a barrage of sharp arrows of criticism, and also in getting his work out there, trying to climb that impossible castle wall of marketing and distribution. In spite of my own anxieties, I admired how he was ready for the challenge. Then, in lucid dreams the castle became death itself, my own human fear of passing over, and his brave wide-eyed fighter's stance. He had perished in a horrific house fire that twisted the steel girders on which the home stood. Could I face death with as much strength as he showed in my dream?

Dreams.

In March of 2013, Kyle and I were talking (in one of our last face-to-face conversations) in his home along Fall Creek in Freeville, New York. He was telling me how he thought that a human's nighttime voyages could be more than a breakdown of past events and a sweeping up of life's daily debris or more than learning about one's character and secret desires. He believed that dreams could be used effectively to reach one's inner creativity and, perhaps, to reach the beyond. I listened politely, careful not to appear overly disapproving of something I felt wasn't particularly plausible.

A little backstory is needed here to appreciate our relationship. It had taken awhile for Kyle and me to get back to just sitting, relaxing, and enjoying each other's company: talking poetry, books, movies, et cetera. He was coming into his own as a man and a writer, and I was slowing down from globe-trotting for my day job. During the first seven years of his life we were very close. I was the zany uncle who would swing him and his younger sister, Kayla, (who'd referred to me as a human jungle gym) high in the air, upside down, and around and around. I even got down on his pre-K level to play in our pretend rock band, The Skeletons. Years later, Kyle would cringe as we'd watch our juvenile performance on primitive VHS video, and I would laugh. In the home movie, he's wearing sunglasses and jamming on guitar, leaping from imaginary heights off his bed to the stage below and continuing to rock on while I banged away, off beat, on a tiny toy drum.

Then, at twenty-three, I entered the Army which was the beginning of a slow separation. As each year passed, my visits back home became fewer and shorter. We knew each other less and less as Kyle was growing into an adolescent. At first, we made idle chitchat, but, eventually, the silence between us filled the all-too-short visits. Our closeness had become a shadow of the days gone by.

In 2010, fate, thankfully, managed to wind back the clock's rusted hands ... just a little. It would never again be how it was, but we did achieve some common ground in books and writers. Kyle introduced me to the work of Vladimir Nabokov and I turned him into a Charles Bukowski enthusiast. Some literary-minded folks might say I got the better deal but not so. Kyle and I were in agreement: a good book was a good book whether it was what is considered literary, pulp, or in the case of Buk, dirty realism. We reveled in talking about Sylvia Plath, J.D. Salinger, and the Beats. I know we were both relieved that the uncomfortable silences were filled with gratifying conversation and spirited discussions. As much as I would like to paint a picture of all sunny days, I can't because, as with most families, it was laced with struggles that barred an unfettered rapport. All considered, in a nutshell, that was our relationship from 1989–2013.

Back to March 2013 and dreams. I listened to Kyle talk about tapping into the undiscovered self and realms through our unconscious voyages, and while I did concede that I believed we can manipulate dreams for our own pleasure and use them to learn more about ourselves, I now know that he gave me a wizened look of, "There's so much more," and we moved on to other subjects.

Sadly, we didn't delve into a topic of common ground: dream journals. I had never mentioned to Kyle that years before I had kept a dream journal, and I didn't learn until after his death that he had also kept one on and off. When my sister, Meta (Kyle's mother), showed me the large stack of notebooks and papers he had left at her house, I dug through finding early poems, letters, and different versions of already published prose as I began preparing his posthumous release, *Celebrations in the Ossuary*. Then, farther down in the box, I came across several battered notebooks. Like an overexcited child, I yelled, "We have his dreams!" It may have sounded foolish in the moment, but for me, as someone who had missed out on so many years of his life, it gave me a chance to discover more about him on a different level—from the surreal dreamscape cultivated under cover of rapid eye movement.

This beguiling world where he lived, loved, fought, escaped mazes, and time traveled was begging to be further explored. Kyle had read the BEAT to a PULP webzine and books, and he was familiar with the work of each writer involved with this collection. With his family's blessing, I called on these friends, asking them to turn fragments of Kyle's dreams into short stories. I picked out a handful of thought-provoking lines (for this first volume: "the lizard's ardent uniform," "the laconic dust," "celebrated stomach of copper" and "two blurry rabbits," "my body was hanging from a conveyer belt meat rack being pulled into a sky," "I sold my soul to the devil for drugs," "a lonely hitchhiker was walking down the road on a sunny afternoon," "I went back in time … and tried really hard to warn him it was the boots that he used to take-off like a space ship"), and I sent off these prompts to each writer along with a bit of insight into Kyle. The rest was up to them to create anything they imagined from the dream prompt, and they all turned in stories I know Kyle would have found positively engaging.

Only after his death did I find out that, like me, Kyle was a fan of *Dr. Who*, and in an episode from season three of the new series, when David Tennant, playing the famous time traveler, says, "Some people live more in twenty years than others do in eighty. It's not the time that matters, it's the person," I think of the twenty-three-year-old Kyle Joseph Knapp and the many lives he lived as a poet, naturalist, musician, son, brother, friend, and dream voyager.

He lived a robust life, and in a way he's continuing to do so ... you're holding the most current example.

I hope you enjoy. He would want you to.

David Cranmer
Freeville, New York
June 2014

"All that we see or seem
Is but a dream within a dream."
—*Edgar Allan Poe*

The LIZARD'S Ardent Uniform

Chris F. Holm

Kyle Williams was sleeping. He was sleeping, and this was just a dream. There was no monster in his backyard.

At least, that's what he told himself—although his eyes told him something else entirely.

His alarm clock glowed 3:17. Kyle's mother had put him to bed nearly seven hours ago. He'd been sleeping soundly until a few minutes back, when he was roused by a short, sharp rap that echoed through the night, and a subsequent lessening of the darkness all around him.

Light, faint and white like the moon's, spilled in through his bedroom window.

But tonight, Kyle knew, the moon was new. It said so on the astronomical calendar that hung above his desk. That calendar, along with his very own reflector telescope, was gift from his father—or, more accurately, a bribe—given to him shortly after they left Boston for Santa Fe.

Kyle's father had been a tenure-track professor of physics at MIT when Ardent Industries came calling, and Kyle himself had been happily ensconced in third grade at The Bellwether Academy, which he'd attended since pre-K. He wasn't present for the phone call, but he remembered afterward listening in on his parents' conversation from the upstairs landing of their Beacon Hill row house, his right cheek pressed against the balusters as he strained to hear.

"Are you sure you want to do this, Eric? Leave MIT? Uproot Kyle?"

"For the chance to have the lab of my dreams, and all the funds I'd ever need to continue my research? For the chance to prove to the world that limitless clean energy is not only theoretically possible, but attainable in our lifetime? Allie, how could I possibly turn that down?"

Apparently, he couldn't, because soon after, they packed their things and drove the family Volvo to their new home—a sprawling ranch-style house on the outskirts of Santa Fe, with russet-colored desert all around. Ardent paid to have their belongings shipped ahead of them, so when they arrived, their furniture was already set up—their dark-stained Colonial pieces looking awkward and out-of-place in this rustic, Southwestern setting. Kyle had barely spoken in the four days it took them to make the drive. He was too heartsick. He missed his old school, his old house, his old life. But when he walked into his bedroom to find amidst his old belongings, a brand new Celestron NexStar SLT Series 130 SLT telescope, his foul mood evaporated.

"I thought you might enjoy that," said his father from his doorjamb with a grin. "You'll see a lot more stars here than you ever could in Boston. Too much light pollution there to make them out, even on a clear night. But way out here, who knows what you might see?"

His father was right. In his whole life, Kyle had never seen so many stars as he had that first night. And thanks to his telescope, he soon found there was more to the night sky than he'd ever imagined. The pock-marked surface of the moon. The reddish haze of the Orion Nebula. The majesty of Saturn's rings. The monster in his backyard.

When that unearthly glow shone through his bed-room window and cast long shadows of his telescope on its tripod, he slipped out of bed and padded, barefoot and pajama-clad, over to the window for a look. What he saw was a beam of light shining down upon a figure in the darkness, some thousand feet of scrub-strewn desert away. At this distance, Kyle could make out nothing of the man—for at that point, he still assumed it was a man—so he aimed his scope in his direction. All he got for his trouble was a blurry mess. But when he dialed back the magnification and adjusted the focus, a figure resolved, standing in an undulating column of white. And that figure was not human.

It *was* human-sized, at least. Somewhere between five-five and six feet, Kyle guessed, although it stood in a strange, feral half-crouch, which made its full height hard to estimate. It had two arms, two legs, and a head, each in the usual place. But its skin—every inch of which was visible, on account of the creature was naked—was plated with thick, green scales like a lizard's. Its hands and feet, while broadly humanoid, terminated in nasty looking claws that glinted like onyx in the strange, pulsing light and seemed capable of retracting at will, because they twitched as if testing the air around the beast, and the ground beneath its feet. Its head, which was tilted to the heavens as though basking in the light's glow, put Kyle in mind of a boa constrictor. Its eyes glistened like puddles of black ink, occasionally clouding over for a moment when the creature blinked—translucent nictitating membranes sliding across its eyes like an eclipse viewed on fast-forward.

When Kyle looked into those eyes, he had a sudden, panicked thought the creature could see him, and he hit the floor. But when his galloping heart slowed to a trot and he screwed up the courage to peek through the eyepiece once more, he realized the lizard-beast hadn't moved: it was still staring up at the unseen light-source high above. Kyle wondered what could possibly generate so bright a beam. He followed the beam upward with his telescope until it dwindled to no more than a single strand of spider-silk bisecting the crushed velvet of the night sky, but he saw no source. He increased the magnification, and the beam widened.

Using that method—an upward tilt until the beam dwindled down to nothing followed by an increase in magnification—he followed the light back to its source, a spinning disc of deeper dark against the starry black. And as he zoomed in upon the aperture from whence the undulating beam sprang, his reflector scope amplifying the light's intensity, a strange sensation overtook Kyle. It began as a hum deep inside his inner ear, a rattle in his molars. And then, at once, he heard them.

No. *Heard* wasn't quite right. It was more like he and they—the creature on the ground, and the one with whom it was conversing on the ship—occupied the same headspace. Ideas flew back and forth between them in a rush, all filtered through the limited experience of Kyle's eight-year-old mind.

From the ship, an interrogative barrage of images. A four-star general, his face unseen, his chest spangled with multicolored medals. A discarded pair of coveralls, plucked off the floor. A policewoman adjusting her belt and putting on her hat.

Did you acquire the uniform?

The beast below's reply registered in Kyle's mind as a box checked on a to-do list, a big thumbs-up, a finish line proudly crossed.

Yes.

The ship, its tone somehow once more questioning: A hand bashing through glass marked IN CASE OF EMERGENCY and retrieving a fire-ax. A cartoon burglar wearing a raccoon-like mask over his eyes and tiptoeing through the darkness, a bag slung over his shoulder. A light bulb glowing ever brighter, and then bursting. Steam billowing from the cooling towers of a nuclear power plant.

What about the ... and here, Kyle's mind struggled to grasp the creature's meaning. It was somewhere between *power source* and *weapon* in his mind. But before he could reconcile the images his brain had been bombarded with, the creature on the ground replied; his

5

mother's kitchen timer approaching zero, a clock just seconds from striking midnight.

Soon.

Then, suddenly, the tone changed. The light grew ... agitated somehow. Angry. Kyle's mind flooded with red-tinted images of an ear pressed against a wall, a TV cop wearing a wire.

They knew someone was listening.

The light blinked out, plunging Kyle into night's full dark. Kyle hit the deck, knocking over his telescope in his haste. A cold sweat broke out across his back and neck. He lay there in the darkness trembling for what seemed like forever.

Helpless. Exposed. Vulnerable.

Eventually, his fear of staying put overwhelmed his fear of moving. He belly-crawled from his spot beneath the window back to his bed, and then—gathering his courage—leapt off the floor, tossing his blankets high into the air. He landed in the boy-sized divot at the center of his mattress as they settled over him.

Kyle lay that way for hours, his fear of the lizard-beast bursting in to find him balanced somewhat by a child's faith in the mystical protection afforded by pulling the covers over one's head.

And then, as the coming sun painted orange the eastern horizon, he slept.

* * *

Kyle tossed and turned well into morning, trying in vain to catch up on the sleep the monster in his yard had stolen from him. He ignored his mother's 8 a.m. urgings to get up, and her attempts to bribe him with chocolate chip pancakes at ten. But it was no use; sleep was fleeting, and when it came, so too did nightmare visions of lizard-beasts hunting for him in the darkness—of spotlights zigzagging across the desert floor as half-seen ships above searched high and low. So instead, he lay beneath the covers, queasy from hunger and exhaustion both, but too frightened to come out.

"I'm worried about him, Eric," said his mother from just outside his door, shortly after her failed pancake bribe. "He's been in bed all morning, and refuses to come out."

"Maybe he's sick."

"He's not, as far as I can tell. His forehead felt normal, and he doesn't sound congested. I think he's ... frightened?"

"Probably just had a nightmare."

"Some nightmare. Will you talk to him?"

A long pause. A sigh. And then Kyle's dad said, "If it'll make you feel better, sure."

Kyle heard, but did not see, the door open. Felt the mattress rock beneath the sudden weight of his father, as he sat down on the edge of the bed.

"Hey, kiddo, you okay?"

Kyle nodded beneath the blankets.

"You know I'd find that more convincing if you'd come out of there."

Reluctantly, Kyle poked his head free.

"Rough night?"

Kyle nodded again.

"Bad dreams?"

"I guess."

"You guess?"

Kyle shrugged. "Seemed pretty real to me."

"You want to talk about it, maybe?"

Kyle shook his head.

"Sometimes talking through a bad dream helps you feel better. You realize how silly it sounds when you say it out loud, and it stops being scary."

He waited, but Kyle said nothing. "Okay," he said, "I won't make you. But your mom's pretty worried about you. You think you could maybe come out and get some breakfast so she knows you're okay?"

"I suppose," Kyle said.

"Attaboy," his dad said, tousling Kyle's hair. "C'mon. I hear tell she's making pancakes."

The two of them walked hand-in-hand down the hall to the kitchen. Right before they entered the room, Kyle's dad exclaimed, "Look what I found!"

For a moment, Kyle had the irrational fear that his kitchen would be full of angry lizard-monsters, all slavering at the chance to sink their teeth into his tender flesh. But when they rounded the corner, there was no one in the kitchen but Kyle's mother. She was mixing up a bowl of pancake batter, and she beamed when she caught sight of him. "Hey, sleepy-head," she said. "You hungry?"

Kyle nodded.

"Good," she said, flicking on the stovetop to heat the skillet. "What about you?" she asked her husband.

"Starving," he said, "but I've got to stop into the lab. In fact," he said, looking at his watch, "I should have been there twenty minutes ago."

"You have to eat," she said.

"I know," he replied. "But I'm already late, and you haven't even started cooking yet."

"Promise you'll grab something on the way?"

"I promise."

Kyle watched his dad lean in and give his mom a peck on the cheek. Watched her fingers graze his chest as he pulled away, a simple gesture of affection. Suddenly, the horrid images of last night that plagued him well into this morning seemed a world away: a bad dream fading into distant memory.

"Later, kiddo," said his dad as he pushed open the screen door and stepped outside.

"Later, Dad!" Kyle called back, smiling.

But as the screen door's old spring yanked it closed, and its wooden frame clacked against the jamb, Kyle's blood ran cold. Because he knew at once that was the short, sharp rap that roused him late last night. That had brought him to the window in the first place.

What did it mean? Had that monster tried to get into the house? He didn't know, but he was sure now what he'd seen hadn't been a dream. Which meant they weren't safe here. Which meant he had to tell someone.

He looked to his mom, but she was busy cooking pancakes, and wasn't paying him any mind. *Not that she'd believe me anyways*, he thought.

But Dad might.

Kyle ran to the screen door. Tried to call out to his dad. But the words died on his lips, and all that came out was a strangled wheeze.

Because as he reached the door, he saw his dad crouched in the driveway like a feral animal, his head tracking slowly from left to right. Kyle followed his dad's gaze, and soon spotted the object that had attracted his attention: a dun brown deer mouse, scurrying across their cracked dirt drive.

As its path across the driveway brought it near to Kyle's dad, his father leapt quick as death, and came up with the squirming rodent in his hands. Then he snapped its neck, and the poor mouse squirmed no more.

And as Kyle watched, he tilted his head back, opened his mouth wide—revealing a second mouth inside it brimming with sharp glinting teeth, like a snake's—and lowered the dead mouse into it by its tail.

Then the thing wearing Kyle's dad climbed into the family Volvo and took off for Ardent Industries, the dirt kicked up by the tires hanging heavy in the air.

†

DUST to Dust

Terrie Farley Moran

The county had long since paved over the main road. Low slung shopping malls and tract houses with two car garages replaced most of the ancient barns and silos that once scattered across the skyline. So much had changed but my mind was stuck on the last time I came down this road nearly forty years ago.

* * *

It was the morning after school closed in the spring of 1963. We left the city before dawn. By first light my father was driving over rutted, dusty roads past ancient farm houses, many needing a coat or two of paint. Riding through the tiny town of Culbertson, not much more than a drug store and a one pump gas station, I started to cry.

My mother reached back and gave my knee a hard smack.

"Stop blubbering. You danced. Now you pay the piper."

Her voice scratched like chalk on a pitted blackboard. My father urged her to shush.

When we got to my grandmother's farm, they dumped me and my scant luggage in Granny's sitting room. My mother sat on a chair in the kitchen and wailed her grievances about how I'd gone wrong as if we were all discovering for the first time why the trip had been made. My Granny fussed around offering sweet tea and promising everything would turn out as the Lord planned. My father had the sense to thank Granny for taking me in. My mother took it as her God-given birthright that her mother would hide the mess I'd made. Soon enough, my mother marched purposefully out the door, announcing that she'd see me when "it" was done and gone. My father stopped to give me a quick hug and whispered. "It'll all be over soon. Pay your mama no mind. We'll visit. I promise."

I spent the first couple of days tossing and turning on the stiff mattress of the single bed in Granny's spare room. When I wasn't sobbing my heart out, I was trying to find a spot where I could wriggle in comfortably. The little monster, as I called it, was growing bigger every day, stretching my belly, taking up room I didn't know I had.

Finally Granny was having no more of my melancholy.

"Come out to the porch," She stood her hands planted firmly on her hips. "You're wasting sunshine, sprawled on that bed, day in, day out." She shook her head. "It's all I can do to get you to eat supper."

That last part was true. My stomach had stopped retching long ago but the smell of most foods still caused the occasional flip flop. I knew Granny wouldn't stop prodding 'til she got her way, so I dragged myself outside and dropped onto the weather-beaten pillows of the porch swing. The overhang shaded my head and shoulders, while my growing belly was warmed by the morning sun. The little monster began kicking as if he was dancing to a tune on the radio.

After a while Granny brought out a bowl of peas for me to string.

"Here you go. Time to start earning your keep." And she plopped the bowl and a knife on the swing next to me.

Even as a little girl I visited Granny's small farm for a few weeks every summer. I'd spend hours running in the fields chasing butterflies in the daytime and fire flies at dusk. Most mornings I'd swim in the pond, really not much more than a mud hole. Afternoons I'd rock in the porch swing, my mind wandering to nowhere and back while I listened to the radio. When I got older, I'd thumb aimlessly through magazines like *Movie Life* and *Photoplay* and imagined my grownup self as a high-fashion model or movie star.

Sometimes Granny would help me build a wood fire in her back yard pit, just east of the vegetable patch. Then we'd hold an old pot with a long handle over the fire and shake kernels of corn until they popped all fluffy and white. Once in a while we'd sit on the porch and take turns hand cranking the ice cream churner. We'd look at the sky and speculate which of the stars were closer to earth and which were further away.

What changed now? How is it I had to earn my keep? I thought about that while I pulled the string on each pod, dropping the peas in the bowl and tossing the pods and strings on the floor to be swept up for compost.

When I finished shelling the peas, Granny brought me a glass of fresh squeezed lemonade and two sugar cookies. She sat in the rocker next to the swing and watched me as I nibbled cautiously always fearful the nausea would return.

"This ain't the worst thing could've happened. You know the Good Book says 'dust you are and to dust you will return.' Lot happens between the two. You're a good girl deep down. Made a mistake is all. No point paying for it all your life. Just move past it. Your mama means well but she's harder on others than she is on herself. Next summer you'll come back and it will all be forgotten.

That was two things Granny got wrong. I never went back, not until today. And I never forgot the humiliation.

The second week, Granny drove me into town. Not tiny Culbertson but the next town over. Bigger, with more streets and more people. And a doctor, an old man whose left hand trembled slightly. He sat on one side of a wide scarred oak desk. We sat on the other. He called Granny "Sarah" and asked about her arthritis.

"Not too poorly. But this here is my granddaughter, the one I told you about. Got herself in trouble."

I dropped my head as far into my shoulders as I could but she went right on talking like I wasn't there. "I need you to take a look, make sure she's doing okay."

He nodded.

"And after?"

"Arrangements all made. Nice couple. Mite old to go through an agency, so we can do this all private like."

"Lawyer?"

"From the City. He'll see it's done legal."

Still nodding at Granny, the doctor turned to me.

"Let's take a look at you.

He walked over to the doorway and called for Louisa. She didn't look much older than me, even dressed as she was in nurse's white.

I followed her to the examination room. She weighed me and then asked how much I'd weighed before. She told me to strip below the waist and handed me a cloth to drape over my lap. She opened the door, nearly stepped out and then changed her mind and closed it again.

"Only sixteen and in the family way? What did the father say when you told him?"

Seeing as how I never did tell Mike Kelly a thing, I had no answer. Mike heard the rumor in school before I'd worked up my courage to say a word to him. He lied all over town saying how I swore I'd done it with a dozen guys before him, and my experience sure showed if the listener got Mike's drift—wink, wink.

So I shrugged at Louisa and shook my head.

I dropped my eyes when I saw the pity in hers.

"Poor kitten. They're gonna take your baby. Well, it'll have a better home than you can give it and I suppose you'll be better off."

Then she waved her left hand in front of my face, and I saw a flash of sparkle float by.

"I tell my boyfriend, Kenny, even this engagement ring don't give him privileges. Boys will take what liberties they can. I guess someone should have told you that before now."

In a few minutes I heard the doctor mumbling outside the door and I wiped the tears Louisa's thoughtlessness had caused.

The doctor poked and prodded for a bit. Then he put his stethoscope in his ears and listened to my ever-growing belly.

He smiled and told me everything sounded good. He called the little monster "the baby" and pronounced it healthy and normal.

Nothing normal about this for me.

We came out of the doctor's office and the bright sunlight hit me, draining the blood from my head. I grabbed Granny's arm. She took one look at my face, declared she'd seen skeletons with better color and walked me right next door into Woolworths. We sat on worn red leatherette stools lining the soda fountain. Grandma ordered me a seltzer, which I obediently drank. After a while I felt stronger and said so. Granny urged me to have something to eat, trying to tempt me with a bacon, lettuce and tomato on toast, my favorite sandwich. The only thing I wanted was to go back to life before. Before Mike Kelly and his sweet talk and groping hands.

When we stood, I noticed the next counter over was stocked with bibs, diaper pins, talcum powder, all the trappings a new baby would need. We passed along, heading for the door and I snatched a green rubber toy, shaped like a pretzel, tiny enough to be gripped by baby hands. I slid it in my skirt pocket. With what I'd already done, stealing was hardly worth a thought.

So the days and weeks crawled by. I went to the doctor another time or two but mostly I sat on the porch, if only because Granny wouldn't let me lie in bed all day. Each afternoon I walked to the mailbox to bring in Granny's mail, her newspapers and such. I'd written letters, made up stories of life in the country and sent them to a few girls from school. Girls I thought were my friends. Not one ever wrote back. I bet they were spending plenty of time talking about me, feeling superior because it was me instead of them got caught.

Summer got hotter. I got bigger. The walk to the mailbox seemed longer.

Some nights Granny would bring the ice cream maker out to the porch and we took turn cranking, while the radio faded in and out with the likes of Tex Ritter singing "I Dreamed There Was a Hillbilly Heaven." If ever the radio man said, "Next we gonna hear Ferlin Husky bless us with his rendition of 'White Dove,'" Granny would clasp her hands, close her eyes and sing along in a reed-thin voice: "A sign from above … On the wings of a dove."

When the music ended she'd rest for a minute and then, like the song was written just for me, she'd say, "The Good Lord's been telling me you'll have a grand life. Just need to get through this is all. One day you'll be an old woman like me and won't hardly remember."

But the day never came when I didn't remember.

I can still feel those pains. No matter I've had three children since. I can still feel those first labor pains. I yelled for Granny and she drove me to the hospital just off Route 40. I try not to think about the rest of that day. Pain followed by more pain and in the end nothing to show for it.

Oh, I had a baby. A baby who was going to grow up as someone else's sweet little girl. I cried, I begged to see her. My parents came, I thought to visit me, but really to sign the papers giving my baby to what mama called "her real parents."

My father kissed me on the forehead and told me it was all for the best. It was my future they were thinking of.

My mother acted like I was invisible. She kissed the air alongside my cheek and was gone, papers signed, her job done.

I lay in bed for three nights listening to babies cry in the nursery, wondering which one might be mine. On the fourth day while she was plumping up my pillows, Granny told me I was going home the next day and asked me what clothes I wanted her to bring in the morning.

"Mind you, everything's not going to fit right away. How about I bring the green plaid jumper?"

I shrugged. Who cared what I wore?

"And the baby?"

When Granny answered, my head snapped up in surprise. It was the first I realized that the question rolling around in my head had been asked out loud.

She patted my hand and told me not to worry. "She's going to a fine home. People got lots of money and a big house. Best of everything for your little girl."

She saw the tears starting and handed me a Kleenex from the box on the night stand.

"Go ahead, have a good cry. I'm taking her to the lawyer this afternoon. Turn her over to her parents all proper like. Then you'll finish growing, have a life of your own. Do anything you want."

She turned to the door.

"Granny, wait. Under my pillow—"

Her eyes took in the pile behind my head.

"Not these. My pillow at home. At your house. I have a baby toy. Little green rubber pretzel. Could you give it to her? I want her to have something from her mother. From me. Something she can keep for always."

Granny's shoulders dropped and her always ramrod spine seemed to collapse. She threw her arms around me and rocked me like I was the baby. Then she smoothed my hair with both hands and kissed me.

"Don't you worry, I'll see she has it forever."

And she hurried out of the room while I pretended not to see her tears.

I stayed at Granny's house another week or two and then my parents drove me home. I was expected to live the rest of my live as though nothing unusual happened that summer. And so I did. Went back. Finished high school, followed by a degree in economics. In graduate school I met Joe, the man I would eventually marry, but not before telling him my dreadful secret. He has spent ages trying to erase my emotional scars and for that alone I will always adore him.

I never came back to Granny's farm. Not once in forty years. Not even when Granny died. Not until this week.

My father's been gone and buried for a long while. Mama died a month ago. September 28, 2001. The entire country was still mourning the attacks on the World Trade Center, so no one noticed how sparsely I mourned my mother. Still, there were legal things to be done. It had finally come as I knew it would, that I was the sole owner of Granny's old farm.

Right after burying Granny, my mother contracted with an old time farmer named Zentz who lived closer to Culbertson. He leased a few acres for crops. As part of the bargain, he kept an eye on the place.

My mother's lawyer advised me to clean out any family bits and pieces and put the property on the market. He said there'd been offers from time to time from developers anxious to build a dozen faux farmhouses with extra size lots for gardening. Joe offered to work with the lawyer so I needn't dredge up the old memories. But I knew I had to take care of this myself. Scare away the ghosts one final time.

I'd spent decades dreaming of burning the place to the ground. When I turned in the driveway and stopped near the rusted out mailbox, I was struck by the deterioration of the house and the outbuildings. The idea of a fire did not seem unreasonable.

I pulled up to the front porch and parked next to a faded blue Chevy Silverado with more than a little mud on the tires. I was glad that Mr. Zentz was already here, cleaning out the barn and stable as I'd directed. I don't care what he did with anything, I wanted everything gone, the estate settled. Then I'd be free of it all.

I sat on the porch steps, not wanting to go into the house. It wasn't long until Zentz, nearly as weathered as his truck, came out of the barn to introduce himself. He thanked me for allowing him the good fortune of having first pick of the farm equipment.

"I'll sell what I can't use. Happy to give you the profit."

I was telling him for what seemed like the fiftieth time that this place had nothing to offer me, when a younger version of Farmer Zentz came running out of the barn with a tattered tan satchel in his hand.

"Pa. Pa. What do you make of this?"

He reached the porch and remembered his manners long enough to tip his hat to me.

"Pa. Look."

He set it down on the ground between his father and me. Satisfied he had our attention, the boy used his kerchief to clear away the layers of dust along the inflexible rim and he pulled the sides wide open. Dust billowed out, as if making room for sunlight that flooded into the bag and reflected on ancient bones. Tiny bones. Tucked among them was a green rubber pretzel.

Granny kept her promise. My little girl still has her remembrance of me.

†

TWIN Talk

Patti Abbott

Wendy came home at six, done-in after six hours of unpacking donations at the Center. There was always at least one "ugh" moment—which was why the receiving clerk was advised to wear gloves. Today, badly stained baby clothes had been pitched into a soggy-bottomed carton. Spit-up, pureed peas, and sweet potatoes, Wendy guessed, tossing the whole thing into a recycling bin. She'd be assigned to some other task after tomorrow, thank God. It was an awful job, paying minimum wage, but the only sort of work available after her previous employer, a fine arts book store, closed overnight.

As she hung up her jacket in the foyer, Wendy could see the girls were sitting on the sofa doing that cat's cradle thing again with a skein of maroon yarn. A pointless exercise as far as she could tell, another excuse to entwine themselves in a way that couldn't be called odd—though it was. It was weird when they were eight, weirder still at thirteen.

Tying knots was another recent obsession. They'd come home from a library book sale with an old Boy Scout handbook and learned to tie each of the fancifully named knots. They'd insisted on buying the recommended gauged rope at a marine supply store, so everything was by the book—or shipshape—as the guy behind the counter said. She'd no idea there were so many types of knots and worried that a future as dominatrices awaited the girls. Where did these interests come from?

Unlike other mothers of teenage children, she'd give anything to have them texting friends, listening to questionable music, watching movies on their phones. The girls didn't need electronic devices to communicate with each other; they didn't even have to open their mouths. It was as if an invisible wire went from one head to the other. What did that doctor call it? Idioglossia? But idioglossia used signs and made-up words. The twins used a sort of telepathic communication. Shaking her head, she ignored their cradling—having been told many times that disregarding it was the best way to handle minor behavioral abnormalities.

"Do I draw the line at knives?" she'd asked only last week. "That's the next chapter in the book. The proper care and handling of penknives. I called the B.S.A. and was told there was no official policy on the use of knives. It appears that camp-crafting is dependent on penknives for various tasks. It's strictly a troop decision. I didn't have the guts to tell the guy it was two girls following the manual—not an official troop."

"The Boy Scout organization dates from a different era," her therapist told her. He had that soothing tone in his voice again. "Pioneering skills were practical a century ago. Many of the kids came from rural areas. They often belonged to the 4-H group too."

Did he really think she didn't know all of this? "Next I think they're on to building campfires. Don't you think all this interest in potential weaponry is leading to something?" She could feel a rope tightening around her neck.

"You're allowing your imagination to run away with you. Save your concern for behavior with a violent or misanthropic aspect to it," one doctor or another (she changed doctors frequently) had told her whenever she mentioned the mind games they liked to inflict on her, or the way she was excluded from their inner lives. There was plenty of worrisome stuff to discuss. She flopped down on his or her sofa once every fortnight and spilled her guts for 50 minutes. Her ex-husband paid for it as part of the divorce settlement. He'd put up almost no fuss when the item "therapy for Wendy" appeared on the settlement papers.

"Don't you think it's the girls who need therapy though?" he asked her. But they seemed quite content in the world they'd created. It was she who suffered from insomnia, anxiety, self-pity.

"Hey, girls! No homework tonight?" she asked with a false gaiety, beginning to remove the items she needed from the fridge. She could swear she'd bought baby carrots, but only a bag of limp regular-sized spears greeted her. The girls only ate certain foods and baby carrots were a staple. Like two blurry rabbits, they dashed back and forth to the fridge all day long loading up on them. She could hear them crunching from their bedroom at night, the sound rising as her insomnia took hold.

"It's Friday," they said in unison, laughing at both her forgetfulness and their spontaneous response. Judith's voice, as usual, was a half-note ahead of Lilith's. She was always the leader, and in the rare instances the two were separated, Lilith seemed unsure of what to do—as if her plug had come undone.

"Of course. Silly old me." Now that she worked six days a week, Friday night had lost all of its meaning.

They looked up for a minute, and she felt their otherness flow across the room. It was like something physical—a current perhaps—and she stepped back. Their faces showed little interest in the object of their gaze—their mother. Their respect had disappeared when their father left, swirling down the drain even more quickly when she took the job as an hourly worker at the resale shop. Wendy looked enviously at mother-daughter duos coming into the store to peruse the racks together. Just the other day, she watched a teenager share a text message with her mother. Oh, for such inclusion. Producing two of them insured her future as a useless appendage.

Teary eyed, she watched her blonde-haired daughters merge in a swirl of late afternoon sunlight and dust motes. They especially enjoyed sitting on that sofa, knowing somehow that the mellow light of late afternoon enhanced their beauty, that the soft apricot fabric was especially flattering. The mirror, on the wall across from the sofa, made their number swell to four. Every few minutes, one or both glanced in the mirror, smiling at what they saw. Wendy wondered what it was like to take such pleasure in your image. Oh, how empowering to be confident of just rewards and certain outcomes. Her mother had drummed such assurance out of her long before thirteen, convincing her that she was careless, untidy, thick-headed.

If Bill were still available for household chores, she'd have him take the mirror down and replace it with her grandmother's wedding ring quilt—a piece of work that reflected a hardscrabble life during the Depression, where beauty and warmth were made with your hands, not found in a mirror.

On learning they were expecting twins fourteen years ago, Bill was so taken with the idea that he tracked down a woman out west who made bronze casts of pregnant bellies. The woman advertised her sculptures as "stomachs of copper" that would be a permanent celebration of the months of pregnancy. They'd sent for the material, called a Mama's Belly Casting Kit, and spent an evening laying plaster strips across her belly. The cast pulled away after a while, and then they packed it up and mailed it off, wrapped in the simple pages of newspaper recommended by the sculptor. Six weeks later, the twins already born, it came back, a copper bowl with a gong. It was grotesquely large to her, never having really seen herself full on. It was a miracle her abdomen hadn't split open like a fallen watermelon.

According to the website, each bowl made a different sound. Theirs was quite deep and resounding. She'd been skeptical, but the bowl was lovely despite its almost macabre presence in their house. She never found a proper place for it so it drifted from the dining room table, to the fireplace, to the coffee table. Sometimes she filled it with flowers; other times fruit. At Christmas it was stuffed with pine cones and greens. But mostly it sat empty now, a sad reminder of the hopefulness from that period of her marriage. Occasionally they'd demonstrate the gong, mostly to explain its purpose to a visitor. Whereas once it sounded reassuring, it now made the loneliest sound she could name.

After studying the literature on twins fourteen years ago, Bill and Wendy decided to dress the girls differently and gave them individual, non-gender specific toys, trying to encourage separate identities. As soon as the twins could remove their dissimilar clothes, they did so, running naked through the house until she gave in and bought the identical outfits they craved. They shared a single toy at a time, passing it back and forth, fashioning clothes for the stuffed rabbit or bear or dog they preferred to play with from the clothing they no longer wore.

Strange incidents and interests were commonplace with the girls. They'd come upon a set of jacks, tucked away in a box from Wendy's mother's childhood, and played the game incessantly between the age of eight and ten. They liked games where they could work together, and if the rules didn't offer that option, they altered them. With the game of jacks, one of them tossed the ball and the other scooped the jacks.

"But you're missing the point," she told them. "It's doing both things at once that's the trick. Whoever picks up the most jacks without dropping the ones in his hand wins."

They looked at her like she was speaking Portuguese.

"Oh, Mother," Judith finally said. "Where's the fun in that?"

Starting very early on, both girls refused to answer to their given names: Charlotte and Sophie. By the age of eight, they'd renamed themselves, announcing they were to be called Judith and Lilith.

"How did they come up with those names?" Bill had asked her. "Wasn't Lilith some horrible creature?"

"Lilith was a demon," Wendy said. "And Judith beheaded a man."

"Nice," he said. "You've got yourselves some girls there."

Bill often ignored his role in the procreation of their children. Sometimes she wished she'd beaten him in his flight—wondering what her life might be like without the girls. But mothers can't do such things without becoming a pariah. And he'd have murdered the twins by now, having only the vaguest affection for his daughters.

"Can someone set the table?" she asked now, turning the skimpy chops over in the pan. Chops like these would never have turned up on her table four years ago. She looked up. "Girls?" she said, raising her voice.

In their former home, one that Bill paid for with his large salary as a trial attorney, it might've taken some time to find the twins, and they might not have heard her call. This house, however, was less than 1000 square feet, and they could hear her bellow from any corner. Sullenly they returned to the room, silently setting the table. How much longer would they even pay attention? Could you make a sixteen-year old set a table if she didn't care to? Lilith perhaps. But never Judith.

But then her mood lifted as she remembered that she had a date tomorrow night. Something good had actually happened. And right at the work place she so dreaded. A nice-looking man came in, carrying several boxes of kitchenware.

"I can get a tax receipt for this, right?" he asked, struggling to lower the boxes without the top one slipping off.

She waved the form at him. "You bet. Just fill this out and I'll sign it."

"Do you guys put a value on the stuff? Is that how it works?"

"No. But you can find a list of the amounts you can claim online," she said. "A general idea of what the government allows."

"It's my mother's stuff," he said when he saw her eyeing a robe. "She died a few months ago, and I am just getting her things sorted out."

"Must be an awful job."

In fact, she knew this to be true. Her own mother had died last year. The hardest chore had been deciding what to do with photographs of relatives that no one, including Wendy, could put a name to. Throwing these photos out, disposing of perhaps the last proof of their existence, seemed wrong. In the end, she shredded the pictures of relatives she couldn't name, along with half the ones she could.

Now that the boxes sat on the table, she could see there was no band on his finger. "Are you doing this all by yourself?"

"Looks like it. My brother's doing the financial stuff. Lena—my sister's—filling out various forms. So I probably got off the easiest." He smiled. "But I'm the one with the muscle."

"I can see that," she said.

Somehow they moved on to a time to meet for a drink after work. She panicked over what to tell the girls. In the four years that Bill'd been gone, she'd never been on a date—or even out much at night with friends. So she lied, telling the twins she was meeting a fellow employee for coffee. They seemed supremely uninterested. A few days went by, and then Craig called her, suggesting dinner on Saturday night.

Friday night dinner with the girls was the silent affair it usually was—with her, unsuccessfully, trying to get a conversation going. If the girls talked at dinner, it was with each other. Wendy was only called upon for money, her approval of a school trip, a car ride to some event, help with a task they couldn't complete on their own. They never shared anything important with either parent.

They put the dishes in the dishwasher while she wiped the counters and table. Finally, in desperation, she turned on the kitchen radio. Her go-to station played music from the eighties, a period the girls loathed. She saw them rolling their eyes.

"Do you mind if I change the station," Judith asked. Before she could answer, Judith had found something unpleasantly riotous, driving Wendy from the room.

Just as life seemed about as desperate as it could be, the phone rang.

"Checking in to see what sort of food you like," Craig said, his voice deep and soothing. Since Bill left, her life was composed almost entirely of sopranos and she'd missed the baritone she now heard.

"I like any food that someone else prepares," she said. Did that sound desperate or funny? There was a line between the two that she couldn't find with a map.

"How about Italian? That's usually a safe bet."

They agreed on a time, and she hung up feeling good. She liked the idea that he'd consulted her before making a reservation. Bill never had—just assuming whatever he liked was appealing to everyone. If he ever thought about it at all.

The phone rang again.

"Listen, can the girls come next weekend instead of this one," Bill said, not bothering with any niceties. "Something's come up."

"This is like the third time this month that you've disappointed them."

"Do you really think they give a shit, Wendy?"

"Actually, I have plans."

Not even bothering to ask what, he sighed. "Look, okay, I'll have to pick them up early though. And I might have to go out for a few hours. They can stay alone, right. They do it all the time after school, don't they?"

"Of course. They are thirteen." Another woman, she thought to herself. He went through women like a horny teenager.

"Last time they were here—well look—is thirteen this witchy with other girls?"

For a split second, she considered asking what they did. But when Bill said the very things that she herself thought, it always made her mad. And this was no exception.

"You know, Bill, both girls feel your disapproval— you give off a vibe—even over the phone." There was a lot more she could say, but she stopped there. One of the doctors had told her that if she stopped speaking— just a sentence or two before she felt finished—she'd avoid airing her most hostile and hurtful remarks. It did work when she could bear to do it.

"You can't tell me they aren't weird. We've known that since they were two. Maybe even earlier. Last time they were here, I caught them performing some sort of ceremony with candles out in the garden."

"They just do it to get you going." At least, she hoped that was true. "Look, at thirteen, I wrote poetry about death. Kids stuck anonymous letters in my locker at school. My mother refused to let me shave my legs or wear makeup. I was the last kid I knew to see "Thriller" on MTV. Thirteen's tough." Wendy remembered applying makeup after leaving the house, but those hairy legs were more difficult to deal with.

"Jeez, if I'd known all this twenty years ago we could have saved ourselves a lot of trouble. I might have still married you, but I wouldn't have had kids." He chuckled. "What were the anonymous letters about?"

What were they about? Maybe her hairy legs. "Oh, just kid stuff," she told him. But thinking back on it, more than one note accused her of being a witch. Some of the kids had called her Carrie, in fact. Had she been as strange as her girls? She wished her mother was still alive to ask. Or had she guarded her secrets as closely as the twins guarded theirs? Her mother had not been the type of woman a teenager confided in. Was she?

"And as for your hairy legs. They kept me warm on winter nights more than once."

Like a heat-seeking weapon, he never shied from the kill. "You did call for a favor, right?"

"Yeah, I'll pick them up right after gymnastics. Still into that, right?"

"It's practically the only time they leave the house."

Both girls were extremely agile so gymnastics made sense. She would've preferred them to take up a team sport—like softball or soccer, but gymnastics was better than nothing. They didn't really care for the competitions though and often claimed to be sick in order to avoid them. Their coach chided her for not pushing them harder.

"They could win trophies at a lot of these meets," he told her. "Boost the program and their team mates."

Wendy didn't care that they didn't care. She was happy to get them out of the house for a few hours three or four times a week. Both girls excelled in the floor exercises and the vault. They'd worked up a joint floor performance, which was strictly illegal according to the International Federation of Gymnastics.

"They allow synchronized swimming in competitions, don't they," Judith said. "I don't see the difference."

"Maybe we should try swimming," Lilith said.

Wendy was about tell them about her high school swim team triumphs when Judith interrupted. "Do you really want green hair, Lil? Or those gargantuan shoulders?"

Lilith looked at her feet as she often did after offering an unsolicited opinion.

After working at the resale shop until noon on Saturday, Wendy dropped the girls off at the gymnastics center, overnight bags in tow, and began a leisurely preparation for her date. It'd been ages since she took a bath instead of a hurried shower. And even longer since she manicured and polished her nails, both hands and feet. She knew in her heart such elaborate preparation spelled letdown, but dolling herself up felt good even if the date detonated. Craig seemed like a decent guy, but she'd heard too many tales from friends on the hunt to not look at the dating scene skeptically.

Craig had already told her he divorced in his late twenties. The woman had married him on the rebound from a soured college romance and then rebounded again. He had no children but adored his nieces and nephews and hoped to have some of his own. He was five years younger than Wendy and never finished college, taking his computer skills to a tech position at a community college.

"I'm taking a course here or there," he told her, embarrassed. "I'd like to design software eventually."

"A lot of good my degree in anthropology did me," Wendy assured him. "I should be back in school myself, getting a skill that's more saleable."

They both shrugged off the other's failures and ordered: Wendy, veal piccata; Craig, the lobster ravioli. Conversation came easily, and she took that as a good sign and invited him back. She couldn't help but take advantage of the rare evening that the girls were not at home.

"Another glass of wine or some coffee?" she asked, pulling out a box of cookies she'd bought on the off-chance things went well.

"Decaf?"

She nodded.

Later she'd remember pouring the coffee and setting three shortbread and three peanut butter cookies on a plate. Craig stood behind her, saying something about the blue of the Delftware plates that hung on the kitchen wall.

"Is that a dinosaur? The one in the middle?"

She swallowed a laugh—about to tell him that the animal on the dish was an elephant—perhaps painted by someone who'd never seen one—when a veil of gray descended. Cotton balls stuffed her ears. This was the way it seemed to her at least. Her legs went numb, her fingers tingled, and that was it.

* * *

Wendy awoke to the resounding sound of a gong. Perhaps a minute has passed. Perhaps hours. She looked around, and the first thing she saw was Lilith, gong still in her hand and the bowl, dusty, but gorgeous at her feet. Where had they found it?

"She's awake," Lilith shouted. "Mother's awake. How do you feel, Mother? No, don't try to sit up yet." She rushed toward her fallen mother, dropping the gong with a clatter.

"Give her a second," Judith commanded from the other side of the room. "Let her breathe."

As Wendy turned her head, she saw something else: a sight that took her breath away. A man's body was sprawled on the floor, tied at every conceivable juncture with a dozen short ropes. A gag was stuffed in his mouth. Duct tape covered his eyes. Her fear that he was dead ended when he shook his head violently.

Her tongue was too thick to talk.

"What is it, Mother? She's trying to speak, Judith."

"Just listen a minute, Mother. We found this slimy guy kneeling over you when we walked in," Judith said. "You were passed out on the sofa. He probably gave you Rohypnol."

"What?" Wendy had found her voice. "Gave me what?"

"It's a date rape drug. We learned about it in Sex Ed."

Wendy considered this idea. Was this something a grown man did? She'd been about to have sex with him anyway. Surely he could sense that. Although perhaps

37

he liked his sexual partners inert. She'd heard of such things."

"Take the duct tape off, girls. Remove that gag."

"He's only going to deny it," Judith said, not moving. "Let's keep him quiet for a second while we think of our next move."

"Lil, take it off."

Her daughter raced across the room, removing it in one swift movement.

Craig screamed for a second or two, trying to push his shoulder up to his mouth for succor.

"Did you slip me a Mickey, Craig?" Wendy asked, not wanting to wrestle with the name of the drug the girls used. She still felt too weak to rise and instead glared at him from her half-collapsed state. "Is that what happened here?"

"God, no," he said after a few seconds. He looked at Wendy. "Are you kidding? What am I—sixteen?" he paused. He turned his head to the girls, standing together in solidarity. "And I'm thinking of filing charges, you two hellions. Your Mom may have been out cold, but I heard enough of your conversation to figure out what went on here."

"We came in, and you were wrestling with Mother on the couch," Judith said piously. "Probably getting ready to rape her."

"You gotta be kidding," he said and turned to Wendy. "They had those ropes all ready. I saw them drag a bag of snakes—I mean ropes—out of their bedroom. They planned this whole thing."

"You were practically on top of her." Judith looked to Lilith for confirmation and received a curt nod. "Deny it!"

"That's true. I was trying to get her to come 'round. I thought maybe it was food poisoning or some sort of female problem." He looked back to Wendy. "My Mom fainted now and then around menopause."

This was the unkindest cut of all. "I am not *around menopause.*"

She detected a blush beneath the ropes. "Well, I guarantee that if a drug was administered it was not by my hand."

"Maybe it was something in the food," Wendy said. "Some sort of allergic reaction. Why don't you untie him, girls, and let him go. How did this happen anyway? Did you wrestle him to the floor?'

She was beginning to have a sense of pride in the girls. Not many thirteen year olds could dispatch a grown man this handily. And surely their actions spoke of some sort of feeling for her. Did they have the ropes ready? If so, they must have sensed her vulnerability and were ready to step in. But being ready to defend their mother and manipulating the situation were two different things.

"They hit me over the head with that damned gong. At least I have a memory of a similar sound. When I came to I was wrapped like a mummy." A twitter from the girls was squashed by Wendy's glare. He put his hand on his head. "A lump, yes."

"I guess there was some sort of misunderstanding here, Craig. Maybe you should just go."

"I'd certainly like to." He wriggled to demonstrate his position.

"Mother," the girls said in unison. "You're going to just let him get away with it."

"You were positively comatose when we came in." Judith's voice was calm, assured.

"Why are you here anyway, girls?" she asked. "What happened at your Dad's?"

The twins looked at each other. "We had bad vibes," Lilith said. "So once he went out, we came right over."

"We took a taxi even. To get here quickly. We both felt something was wrong and we turned out to be right. He was all over you, Mother. Had a hand down your blouse. Your skirt was up around your waist."

"I was unbuttoning your top button to see if that helped," Craig said. "I was seconds away from an emergency call. Look girls, grown men don't use drugs like that one. What woman wouldn't report him afterward?"

"If she even woke up," Judith said. "If your heinous plot didn't include her death."

Although it was unclear whether or not Judith was correct, Wendy couldn't help a grin.

"I think if Craig had given me a serious drug— like—"

"Rohypnol," her three companions said together.

"Right. Well, if he had, I doubt I would feel right as rain already. So let's unloosen him, please."

Making the same face, the two girls began their task.

"It might go quicker with a knife," Lilith said, hopefully.

"No," both Craig and Wendy said together. Within a few minutes, Craig was gone, shaking his head and muttering something about crazy women. Something about witches or perhaps, bitches.

Wendy knew she should be angry and deliver them the lecture of a lifetime. But all she could concentrate on was that her girls had saved her from what they thought was a threat. Now the three of them would be as close as the mothers and daughters she admired in the shop. The ones at the mall, the ones at the movie theater, chuckling over a rom-com.

"So they'll be no more of that, right Mother?"

"What?" she asked coming out of her reverie. Both girls stood in front of her, their eyes hard. "No more of what?"

"No more picking up strange men and bringing them into our home." Judith's voice was as stern as hers might have been if she'd chastised them properly.

"I hardly picked him ..."

"The next time we may not get here in time," Lilith said. "We can't always be on guard."

"Or we may not want to," Judith said. "We only have so much ... patience."

In a minute, the girls had gone off together, shutting their bedroom door firmly. She heard the crunch of carrots, the sound of a shared giggle. She was alone again—any idea of a change in the climate, squashed.

In the mirror across from the apricot sofa, she barely seemed to exist at all. It seemed like those two blonde heads were imprinted on it somehow—a permanent discolor. Perhaps she was slowly disappearing as their image achieved dominance. She'd look for that wedding ring quilt tomorrow—before it was too late.

†

The MALIGNANT Reality

Evan V. Corder

Flickering phantoms, winking in and out to the eye. Two of them propelling toward me, fast, like bullets from a chamber. I've seen them several times now, and though the 'faces' seem familial—like expressions in an old photo album—I can't get a fix on them. Whenever the phantoms appear, they are always leap frogging in accelerated time, circling me. Initially, I thought the flickers were remnants from my LSD days. A kind of lucid nightmare my mind is manufacturing, mystic delusions of some kind. Of course, I'm not losing it if I know I'm losing it. That much I do know.

As they close in, a whispered, gibberish chant passes between them, "Eraweb Fo Elbon, Eraweb Fo Elbon."

I hurry across the century-old red bricks of Ithaca, the apparitions flanking to my left. I misstep and splay headlong onto the hard asphalt and, almost simultaneously, hear college girl laughter. I push-up from the pavement, picking up the pace, heading past the shops that make up The Commons and slip into a cloistered passage between a bank and used bookstore.

Slouching—preposterously trying to blend—
behind a gutter drain, peering around to see if they've
pursued. *This can't be residue from a bad trip.* No.
More like reality's structure has been bent to the point
of exhaustion. I turn, seeing a lone presence I hadn't
noticed. Against the wall, at the far end of the alley, an
old man wearing a puritan hat. A quirky staple about
town. He's holding on to his ever-present, gnarled
walking stick, observing me with apparent amusement.
Above him on the bank's parapet my assailants
materialize. I lunge in the other direction, muscling my
way through an "Employee's Only" door—into the
bookstore's stockroom.

"Just passing through," I assure a startled, young
worker who's rolling a joint and continue on deeper into
the establishment. I cut around customers perusing bargain books to the checkout, craning my neck from
corner to corner of the front window trying to get a
glance of the bank's rooftop.

"May I help you?" a wall-eyed blonde demands
with annoyance at my nervous squirrel routine.

"Do you see them?" I ask.

"Excuse me?"

"Look. On the roof."

She steps closer, places a hand on a stack of J.K.
Rowling's and scans the skyline. "I don't see anything,"
she snips.

I glimpse again. She's right. Nothing.

"If you're not buying anything I have to ask you to
move aside for paying customers."

I check over my shoulder but there's no one in line. As I turn back around, my eyes fall to a book on false awakenings. "I'll take this," I say, digging into my pants pocket and pulling out a crumpled twenty dollar bill.

"Good choice. I have that dream book too."

I smile as she hands me change and the bag, making one last look outside. It's presently void of hostile gargoyles so I take my leave while it's clear.

* * *

I'm clutching the package, crinkling the inadequate comfort object hoofing it down the sidewalk. I had parked my car three blocks, retracing my steps that started this day with no remembrance of where I was headed. This, of late, has become an uncomfortable reality: circumstances stringing me along, a back seat driver with no control.

A blur of students, business rubes, and homeless as I zig-zag my route. Not looking back nor to the side. Self-imposed blinders. I sense the evil breathing down my neck. Still hear that susurration, echoing, "Eraweb Fo Elbon."

I leave The Commons, ignore the flashing Do Not Walk sign. Finally, my Ford Taurus is in view, parked in front of Mayer's Smokeshop & Newsstand. A sharp reflection of light from a passing truck casts a blinding palm over an ebon shape straight in front of me. Salvation in a traditional habit dress, sent to protect me? Silliness but for that briefest of instances, I was willing to sign away a lifetime of pious doubt to accept a little assistance from the good sister. The vehicle passed as did the hope. Her saintliness was of the Princess Leia variety standing next to a Wookie. A day before Halloween and already reveling.

I roar the Taurus to life and pull away as fast as I can. Is there a chance my roving demons are earthbound tricksters? In the rear view mirror, an answer, at least a hundred feet in the air, I catch a better glimpse of my stalkers, their mouths warped in Munchesque screams.

* * *

I'm at my friend Fox's house to hit him up for some of his ostensibly endless supply of heroin. He never goes out of his way to offer it, but it's always there.

I clear a spot on the over-worn couch and sit. Leaning forward, I put my elbows on my knees, clasp my hands together in front of me, and take a look around the cramped room. He works nights stocking shelves at Walmart, and I don't get how he's able to afford all the smack.

"Man, where do you find the money?"

"I have a contract with Mr. Noble."

"*Noble.*"

"Yeah. You know, the old guy that hangs out at the bars 'round town."

I lean back on his couch, stretch out. "You mean that Aleister Crowley wannabe who carries a skull-knobbed cane? I saw him not too long ago trawling in an alleyway like he was lining up fresh recruits."

"That's him." Fox laughs, reaching for his needle. "He believes he harvests souls or some horseshit like that." I glance past Fox. The bustling Monday soldiers heading to a gloom-and-doom existence come in frame of the picture window then leave. No signs of supernatural assassins. Not for a week now.

"But where's the junk come from?"

"Dunno. Noble arranges it. Package shows up on cue once a month. Before George died—" at the mention of that name, we both throw a two-finger salute templeward to a snapshot tacked on the wall next to an Arak Brandy ad. George's childlike features uplifted into a brilliant smile, arms draped over the shoulders of two stunning stoned blondes on each side of him. He died a year ago of heart failure.

Fox lowers his hand. "He told me about Noble's contracts and hooked me up."

"This set-up for anybody?"

"Don't see why not. He seems to prefer young people."

"Sounds kinda twisted, amigo."

"Maybe. But who's borrowing from who?" Fox rolls up his sleeve and ties off his arm, looks for a good vein. "I think he just likes being seen having a beer with a young crowd. His boys, as he calls us. Makes him feel youthful again, I think. That's all. He has old money to burn. Never asks for anything in return." Fox pushes the needle into his skin, and, a few seconds later, his eyes roll back in sweet abandon. "C'mon, Poet. Give me some of your lyrical wisdom."

"Sure, Fox. How 'bout this latest one I'm calling "the needles."

kissing heads of familiar transition
the claiming stretches of phalanges
into the skins
pushing forward, begin

the procedures of the empty trenches
snow white servants with robes and wrenches
into the skin
swimming sodomy of the pins

He smiles, "Must be nice. Summoning ... arranging words ... at your beckon call."

"They're over-embroidered by a stitch or two. You're just an easy audience."

"Now ... now ... no reason to insu—"

"Dream on," I whisper, yanking out my last Marlboro Red, setting it alight. I've decided against tripping for the time being, but watching his joy reminds me of the William S. Burroughs passage, "Here time has little or much influence. A million years can pass in an injection, an orgasm, a glimpse of 'pure lyric happiness'." Or was it Paul Bowles?

* * *

The bartender sets another Jack Daniels in front of me and a water in front of Noble.

"When you come from a warm climate like I do, you learn to hydrate. Helps against a hangover." He raises his glass with a wink and takes a swig.

At the bar's counter, up close, Noble has a strange appearance. His eyes seem different, drained.

"You want a contract, then?" he asks.

"No strings attached, I was told."

"That's right, no strings."

"Whadda I have to do?"

"Nothing. Or, rather, next to nothing. Let me explicate ..."

Noble's spindly fingers are still wrapped around his glass of water as he continues to dribble on, slow and deliberate. I hear his words, but I'm distracted—my thoughts steal back to his peculiarity. The fingers are seemingly too long, even for a concert pianist if that's possible, and the bones beneath the skin of his hands bellow out to be released from the taut casing that contains them. Sunken-in cheeks give way to an old maid's mouth. Grounding his tapering face is a pointed chin. Wide nostrils flare on his thin, razor-straight nose. And his eyes, set too far apart, appear to move independently of one another, almost like a chameleon.

The strangest part is that none of this really is all that remarkable if you're not paying close attention; it's only noteworthy because I'm bothering to emphasize the oddity of the man up close. All the same, Mr. Noble could pass you on the street and you wouldn't give a second look save for his puritan hat straight out of Robert E. Howard and his novelty-store skull cane that the eyes light up when Noble gets particularly animated and shakes it.

I'd say I was listening to his 'nobleness,' but since Fox had me the day before at free drugs, Mr. Noble's words of explanation were superfluous, and I suspect he knew he already had an enlistee.

"So, am I invited inside your house?"

"Yeah, whenever."

His pale, bony claws release the water glass on the bar countertop and clasp my arm. "I asked. Am. I. Invited ... *Inside*?" His stern, narrowed eyes focus squarely on me, then give way to the beatific smile, returning in full force, acting like a used car salesman before the buyer's signature is scrawled down.

"Kinda cliché, aren't we?" I avoid adding 'for a devil' but I could tell he knew it was implied despite that his pasted on smile held. "Okay, whatever, you are invited to my house and come *inside*. Have a cup of coffee. Sit on the couch and kick your feet up on the table and watch TV. Good?"

He backs off, clutching his cane. "Very good ... very satisfactory." His eyes dart to the glowing sockets of the cane's head.

* * *

I turn off Mill Street onto the long gravel driveway lined with a row of tall pine trees, and I park next to the mobile home that sits about 100 yards from the peaceful sounds of Fall Creek in the pastoral outskirts of Freeville. It's more than just a trailer, it's the home that once belonged to my grandparents, lovingly cared for by the both of them for nearly fifty years. That's before Grandpa died from complications following a stroke, and then a decade later, when my grandmother's Alzheimer's was undeniable, she was shuffled off to a nursing home in Texas—against my protests. And that's when I moved in, inheriting Grandma's orange and white tabby, Sammy the Cat, with the house.

I walk the pathway to the side door, stepping on a blanket of rust-colored pine needles and fallen cones that crackle under my feet. It's an Indian summer day in Upstate New York and I inhale a deep lungful of warm, earthy air. The haze in the sky is typical for this kind of autumn day but not rain, yet I can feel it's on the way ... I can smell the moisture in the air.

The trailer is not so much to look at, that is, unless it's one of the first places you laid your eyes on as a kid and played there with your sister growing up. Then it takes on another entity and becomes home. I feed Sammy and grab a bottle half full of Arak Brandy and flop on the couch. I slow on the junk—getting low—Mr. Noble is making his Grand Poohbah visit tonight.

I leaf through my new book, finding an interesting factoid that the six to twelve minutes after the body has died, the brain is still flourishing. Enough time to live an entire life again.

After a time, a car pulls in the driveway. It's gotten dark outside, and I can't make out who's here—I gotta replace the spotlights.

It must be Noble, and I admit I'm a bit anxious as I head to the car to greet him.

As I walk up to the classic Oldsmobile 88 convertible, I relax when I see my friend Aiden behind the wheel, a girl sitting close to him on the bench seat.

"What do you think of my new ride, man?" Aiden asks.

"Nice," I say, nodding my head. "What are you doing driving around with the top down? It's supposed to rain."

"*What?* You're crazy, man, it's a perfect night," he says, ignoring the cloudlets forming. "C'mon, get in. I'm taking Anna for a ride to Buttermilk Falls."

I look at Anna and smile at her, and she smiles back coquettishly.

"Nah, I can't. I got someone else dropping by soon."

"Don't be such a drag. I'll have you back in an hour."

Anna snugs up even closer to Aiden, and pats the seat next to her.

A godlike snap of thunder roars. I look up, shaking my head, when I see the phantoms coming closer.

I throw open the car door and squeeze in the passenger side. "Let's go!" I say, not letting on about what I'm witnessing.

Aiden tears out of the driveway and down the street. "Where have you been anyway?" he asks. "I've been trying to get a hold of you for a while."

I rub the stubble on my chin as I check the rearview. The flickers are closing in on the bumper, one demon has an outstretched staff like he's aiming a weapon.

"Shit!" I say out loud.

"What?" Aiden says. "What's the matter with you?"

"Nothing. Hey, how fast can this old rattletrap go?"

A sly grin passes over his face as he stomps on the accelerator. The trees along the road are whipping by in a blur and tangles of dead leaves on the shoulder of the road are being kicked up. I look over to see Anna white-knuckling the sleeve of Aiden's jacket. The ghosts fall back but regain their momentum as the Olds goes into a curve then straightens out.

The car hits a frost heave and we bounce up off the seat. I thump my head into the raised visor, and as I'm coming down, I look over to Aiden and Anna. But they aren't there. Jackson Pollock, the artist himself famous for his drip-style paintings, falls into the driver seat where Aiden was and Anna is vaulted into the back seat. For a moment, we're careening out of control on a curving Long Island road, when the lane turns into a familiar route nearer to home, by Cornell University. I'm reeling from the wild ride and Anna is clutching the backrest of the front seat. Around a final bend we plow straight into the stone wall for the university. Anna screams "NO!" just before impact.

I'm not wearing a seatbelt and my body begins grinding movie slow-mo through the dashboard. I can feel my body working its way through the console and then the engine but there is no pain. Passing over. Floating upward and away from the car. I look back to see my listless figure crumpled on the floor. I hear the girl yelling for me to stay "with her." Pollock is gone and being carried away by two flickers but not my own. I'm angling toward my two handlers who are hovering above me in the sky and their faces are just now becoming recognizable when I hear Anna yell my name.

I'm hurtling back. Grabbing handfuls of air. Time to wake-up. Swimming back to the life. Fighting to remain.

The book on dreams drops to the floor. Sammy is perched on the armrest observing me with cold feline bemusement. I check my watch. Seconds. A trickle of moments. I try to switch the light on but must have blown the bulb. I feel my way into the bathroom and douse my face with water.

Stay awake, motherfucker, I tell myself. I turn on the television and flip the channels. It blots out the sound of the soft droplets pelting the roof. I stop on an old film. Forgotten actors to entertain my fading day, walking through their black and white landscape, lower my resolve once more.

* * *

"Perchance to dream," a voice calls out. A silhouetted Hamlet appears before me.

"Asleep or not asleep?" the Prince of Denmark sneers while creeping around my couch. Long, gangly fingers reach over me as the shadowed prince morphs into a hairless Nosferatu.

Did I really invite a stranger into my house? To collect my soul? Absurd.

I see the ghoul's outline cast against the dancing hues of the television screen. A dank wet smell compresses the room as the shadow settles into Mr. Noble's illuminated pallid face.

I'm caught in a schizophrenic trance of some kind. Thoughts are passed by Noble's voice. Many times faster than usual, maybe six times normal cognition. Repeating and revising some algorithm, something to do with death. A doctor, dressed in black hovers over me, filling an opening in his cane with my blood. My mind reaches back to those flickering apparitions— souls inside the skull—the devil's own lantern.

"Eraweb Fo Elbon!" My mind grinds over like tumblers of an unused lock. BEWARE OF NOBLE.

I surge up, hitting Noble. Flesh into sickening, cold marble. I punch him again. He doesn't budge. I roll sideways to get away. "Fuck you!"

"Your soul is mine!" His shadow thunders as he billows in height until his ghost has spilled to every corner, enshrouding the room. An animal stench washes over me mixed with a smell of sulfuric corrosion. And another smell: blood. My blood, dripping from the cane and finding a tributary along his elongated fingers and down his wrist.

Drops of sweat bead on my forehead. "I didn't agree. To this."

"Oh, yes," his gravelly voice spits out the words, "but you did." The last of my blood that he had collected seeps into the vial. He moves the container to his vest pocket, tapping it down in.

An explosion of light blinds from outside my windows. A blink of an eye transformation as dyed yellowish silver swarms my house. Wind bursts through the window, opening it with pounding force and smashing a table lamp to the floor. Noble's shadow collapses to appropriate size. He grasps his cane a bit more secure. The eyes of the skull top, which had been vibrantly illuminated, darken.

"Your master must be bored this evening," Noble taunts outwardly into the waves of blackness.

There's no audible answer, but I detect a conversation is going on. Low, almost undecipherable hums lifting and then dropping away.

And time is at a standstill: brave Sammy slowly in mid-retreat, the rain's droplets like hail now frozen as they entered the open window, and a sense that we are far, far away from New York. It was my narrow living room, but it wasn't. Not anymore. We're a million years in the past, in the drenched lands of earliest evenings.

Whoompf!

A reddish burst of energy erupts from Noble's cane. Surrounding almost everything leaving only me and two opposite corners of the living room untouched. The 'others' don't appear to be fighting back. Just protecting and keeping Noble's anger sequestered.

"What's so special about this one?" Noble snarls, a look of loathing contorts his features.

Another short blast from Noble's cane is deflected inches from my head and fades away in a shower of sparks. Two hooded priest-like figures are transfiguring, each holding a wooden staff in a horizontal position in front of me. The flicker phantoms that have been following me. My hand reaches out to touch—nothing. More booms from Noble's cane, bouncing harmlessly off their gnarled wooded staffs and spinning away into thin air.

"Using those abooghanys won't stop me forever." The tendons of Noble's neck cables like a frilled lizard's hood. Both of Noble's hands grip his cane aiming the skull dome directly at me as the hooded defenders raise their staffs higher to a more strategic position. Another hellish gust of energy hurtles toward us and is collected on the tips of their abooghanys. Swirling dynamos of electricity and light.

Bit by bit, my guardians lower their staffs and Noble's own energy rebounds back, hurtling him against the book shelves in a clattering din. One of the flickers steps forward with outstretched arm and the vial of my blood floats out of Noble's inside pocket, hovers over the demon's head and pops, raining crimson.

I fall back through the shifting sand of centuries to my adjoining dining room table, fumble a cigarette from the pack on top, and light it. Soothing savage nerves and peering through sulfur fumes I gamble, "What fun is it to collect from an unwilling participant? Where's the challenge, mister *ignoble*?"

The old man gradually rises, brushes his clothes, and extends his right hand. His cane rushes to his waiting clutch. His posture relaxes, with chin to his chest, his gaze skims the room, settling on an exposed weakness, the bottle of Arak Brandy that I left on the floor by the couch. He smirks as a cigarette from my pack crosses the room, lights en route, to his waiting lips. He inhales with religious fervor. "One way or another. We'll uphold this contract, young man."

His disconcerting smile remains plastered as his lean figure snaps apart in a swirling fairy-tale smolder and evaporation. The two flicker phantoms, my two heroes, turn toward me. Familiar movements, both. Friendly warm smiles, from a photo—the pictured past— taken long ago when we were all still full of life. Fox and George. I blink, and they're gone.

The conversation with Fox had seemed real enough but was, in fact, REM sleep. Fox had died like George of heart failure before his twentieth birthday.

After a time, I retire to the porch, my small writing alcove that I've dressed to write letters and poems and to sort my problems. I salute the picture of me, George, and Fox taped to the right of my desk. I begin by typing into my journal, *I had a dream I sold my soul to the devil for drugs.* Sammy the Cat wanders into the bower, leaps onto the table, and waits to be petted. I oblige. "Real brave there, buddy."

On the skyline, a gray horizon turning to blue in the cold morning haze.

I crack my knuckles over the keyboard, and I begin typing again, hammering away rather, finishing up recording these latest dreams.

I hear a sudden chortle and look up. Noble's face pushes up close to mine. I shove the swivel chair back and the malignant grin—a projection—disappears.

Another dream?

I take a swig of brandy, calming myself, trying to ignore my overactive imagination of friends departed and demons—like the outline of wet footprints from the passed storm, fading like a bad dream, on the wooden floor.

✝

GHOSTS in the FOG

Steve Weddle

A woman from the ambulance stepped toward me. "You might want to sit down and let me check that." She was looking at the side of my forehead. I pressed my palm against it, felt bits of something pressing sharp pain into open flesh, like a clumsy root canal. She pulled my hand away, worked latex fingers into my face, pulling out bits of ground, shards of gravel. In a couple of minutes I was leaning down in the back of the ambulance while she squirted a bottle of something into my forehead, blotting it with gauze, flesh tender.

* * *

They sewed me up pretty quickly once I got to the ER, put a bandage on my forehead, up near the corner. If I still had hair there, it might have been a problem. I put the paperwork they'd given me in my pocket. Then I signed some other papers at a counter and asked about Brent.

"Brent Rumbelow?" she asked.

I nodded.

"And your name?"

"You just had my name. On all the forms you just did."

"I apologize for the inconvenience, sir, but I am in a different screen now."

I wondered how many responses she had memorized. I told her my name again.

"Yes. I have the record here, but I can only release that information to his next of kin."

Brent's parents had been killed in that small plane crash outside Denton a few years back. It was on the news, our sophomore year of college. He didn't have brothers or sisters that I knew of. "Who is that?"

"Well, sir, I can only release that information to his next of kin."

"You can only reveal the next of kin to the next of kin? Can you just tell me where my friend is? Is he at this hospital?" I wheezed a little, heavy in my chest and could feel the skin on my forehead, the skin they'd deadened before, tingle with heat, tender flesh on display. "Can you just tell me that?"

"Only if you are his next of kin, which," she dragged a finger along the screen, "it appears you are."

"I am?"

"Yes, Mr. Crawford. Your cousin is in O.R. number three. That's on the second floor in the Louisiana Farmers' Credit wing. You can take the elevator at the end of the hall to the O.R. waiting room."

I turned away.

"Is there anything else I can help you with today, Mr. Crawford?"

* * *

The woman at the information desk on the second floor said that Brent had been in the O.R. for about an hour. She said I could sit in the waiting room and someone from the trauma team would be in to update me soon. Then she handed me a beeper and a voucher for a meal in the cafeteria. "We'll let you know if anything changes," she said. "Is there anything else I can help you with today, Mr. Crawford?"

I sat down in the waiting room. Television turned to the news. A window with cheap blinds bent and broken, looking onto another wing of the hospital ten feet away. A chip machine. A coffee machine. Brent's new girl-friend wearing a pink T-shirt and jeans, sitting on a couch and reading a gossip magazine.

She stood up. "Danny?"

"Hey. When did you get here?"

"I got the call about Brent. How is he?"

"I don't know," I said, touched my head, leaned back in the chair. "What did you hear about Brent? They just told me he was in O.R."

"Cop I know called. Said there was a shooting at Adams Creek. What happened?"

"He came with me to talk to the guy over on Merganser."

"The squatter?"

"I don't think he's a squatter. I think he used to live there. Think we all scared the hell out of each other."

"He had a gun?"

"Yeah. Pistol. Little thing. I mean, whatever that matters. I don't know. But it was little."

Angie shook her head. "What were you two thinking?"

"Well, somebody had to do something."

"Not this." She waved an arm around the room.

"No," I said, took a breath deep enough to feel the pain. "I guess not."

Angie and Brent had been going out for a year or so. There'd been another between her and the ten years he'd spent with Bonnie. I'd liked Bonnie.

A woman in blue scrubs walked into the room. "You here with Brent Christopher Rumbelow?"

I said I was, leaned forward, told her my name. Angie said her name.

"They're still working on him. He seems to have a metatarsal fracture. Some bumps and bruises. The problem seems to be the comminuted fracture in the left forearm. He's in surgery now. We'll know more soon."

"Fractures?" I asked. "That sounds like it could have been worse."

"Well," she said, "it's not good. But yes. It could have been worse. I suspect he'll need to stay in a plastic cast for the next six to eight weeks for his foot. A hard cast for the arm for a little longer."

"OK."

"Is there anything else I can help you with today, Mr. Crawford? Ms. Raymond?"

* * *

Angie and I walked down to the cafeteria for some coffee.

Neither one of us wanted to talk about Brent's surgery, about what was happening at the moment. I said something about the coffee being too weak. She said something about the chairs being ugly.

She set her cup to the side. "You want to tell me why you and Brent were at some homeless guy's house?"

"He's not homeless. Not if that's his house, I mean. We wanted to talk to the guy there. Or see what was going on. I don't know."

"Why didn't you just call the cops?"

"We did. I mean somebody in the neighborhood did. Couple weeks ago. Didn't find anything."

"So you guys decided to play cop?"

"Just thought we'd go see if anyone was still living there."

"Guess you got your answer."

"Yeah."

"Why you? I understand why Brent goes, because you asked him and he's your BFF or whatever. But why you and not someone closer?"

"I don't know. There's families around. There was some talk at one of the neighborhood meetings. The one with the bylaws they were writing. Everybody was saying nonsense. I just thought I'd go and I guess I said something to Brent while he was over playing Call of Duty and we just figured we'd run up and check it out."

"Drunk?"

"No."

"Drinking?"

"Yeah. Probably. Not drunk."

"Jesus Christ, Danny. You looking for a story? Get back into reporting? That what this is about?"

"No, that's not what this is about. We just were going to check it out. Look. See if somebody needed to do something."

"Somebody who? Somebody you?"

"No," I said. "I don't know."

"So, you guys play this video game all day about killing people and then just decide to waltz on up and have a nice chat with these, these whatever, these squatters?"

I shrugged. "I don't know. Something like that. But better. It was just the one guy anyway."

"Let me guess. You wanted to be a cop when you grew up? Not a reporter. A cop?"

"I never wanted to be an astronaut or cop or anything. Helmets and spaceships." I tilted my coffee cup on its edge, trying to get the coffee that was left to level off, to stop moving. "Never thought about growing up and doing that."

"Then what?"

"I don't know."

"Just tell me, Danny." Her voice pitching up. "What did you want to be when you grew up?"

"Who cares?"

"I'm just asking you a simple question. You wanted to be a cop when you grew up, didn't you? So you go off playing cop with Brent?"

We watched a nurse in green scrubs push a little boy in a wheelchair past a few tables until the mother caught sight of them, rushing to hug the boy, the dad standing back, dragging his fingertips along the table top.

"No," I said. "I didn't want to be anything. I just wanted to be older."

The father was making that smile, tight in the lips, wrinkles in the forehead. The kind where you're standing back a little, waiting for someone to tell you what to do.

"It's like this catalog we had in college," I said. "We used to get in the mail. Where you can get D.H. Lawrence's shoes for $200. How they tell that story and you're walking through the light rain in Ceylon and this woman knows your name and then she takes you to a room over a café and someone is playing violin and you watch the moon between the buildings and everything is just right and whatever. I wanted that. Whatever that is. Not a job."

She nodded, started to smile a little. "You should get those shoes."

"Yeah."

She sat there for a minute, and neither of us said anything for a while. "So why did you want to be a reporter? Stories like this?" she asked.

I didn't know if she was just trying to make small talk or if there was some fiendish plan. But I didn't want her yelling at me for nearly getting her boyfriend killed, so I was fine with this. We could talk nothing all day. Just go along with it, until it's time to leave. Just step onto the moving floor, hold the handrails, let it carry you along. "Hell if I know. Why'd you want to be a lawyer?"

"You first."

I pushed the handle of my mug, moving it around on the table. "I don't know. I guess because I was good at it. Or thought I was."

"You did the crime beat when you started?"

"A little of everything, like everyone else at the paper. Started doing courts and sports."

"Weird mix."

I shook my head. "Not really. You sit in the audience. Write up what happens, the big plays. Tell who wins. Get post-game quotes from the lawyers, coaches. Just sit back and watch."

"And that's what you liked? Sitting in the audience and writing?"

"Yeah. Then I did some business writing. Some political stuff. You know, where the funding comes from. Who the players are."

"More like courts and sports?"

"Yeah," I grinned, forgetting for a second everything else that was going on, falling into talking about something that made sense, that I could hold on to. "I liked writing the stories. Getting the information together. Looking at all sides and finding out what's really going on. What makes sense. Seeing how things work, you know? How they fit together. How they could work better. Like the consulting I do now."

"Corporate business? Doesn't sound like much fun to me."

"Takes a certain kind of mind. Analytical. You look at spreadsheets. Cashflow. Make sure folks are putting their money where they can make more money. You lawyers probably do the same sort of analysis in seeing what fits and what doesn't."

"I've had a couple of cases that required substantial business expertise, I suppose. Derivative contracts. Retained earnings."

"Yeah," I said. "What I do isn't that complicated. Sometimes I just say 'online strategy' for a couple of days until the check clears."

She nodded for a second, then tilted her head again and looked at me as if for the first time. "You ever think about being an attorney like your father? I studied some of his cases at LSU."

I pushed my chair away from the table a little. "I wouldn't have been like my father."

"No. I don't suppose so," she said, and I wasn't sure what she meant. "Geez. Didn't mean to bring you down. He's been gone how long? Little over a year?"

"Eight months," I said.

She nodded. "I was just wondering whether reporting or defense law is easier."

"The judicial or the journalism?"

She grinned. "Right. You said you had to look at all sides. Defense looks at all sides, but only has to present the one."

"Well, but you still have to know both sides. You have to know what the other side has. What they're likely to spring on you, right?"

"Oh, sure. And it's tough having to fight, to pour your soul into something and then not come out with what you wanted."

"You think reporters don't do that?"

"You play both sides, right? Never have to worry about being on the losing side?"

"I've lost before," I said. "It's overrated."

I refilled our coffees from the counter and sat back down.

"It's not so much the playing both sides," I said. "It's looking at the sides, being objective. Being able to hold opposing viewpoints in your head. Just looking there at both sides."

"Holding everything and touching nothing?"

"What's that mean?" I asked her.

"Something my mother used to tell me. About not keeping yourself out of the world. Not thinking you were better than everyone else. Being able to be involved in things. Not being a ghost in the fog."

"Being involved. Right. That always works out well. Look at Brent."

"You can't completely blame yourself for that. I was giving you hell before, but it's not like you pulled the trigger."

"I don't know."

"It will be fine," she said, leaning in like she was going to touch my hand, my arm. She didn't. "He'll probably have some pain killers. Extra couch time. He'll be fine."

"It's not that," I said. "I mean, I know he'll be fine. But I've just been replaying it in my head. Not of Brent getting shot at, getting hit or whatever. Not of me falling down the stairs." I scrunched my eye to see if my head still hurt. It did. "I have the image of that second before we went in, you know? Like, if we'd just walked away, I don't know."

Her shoulders were down now. She was nodding as I talked. "I guess you guys were just trying to help." She said it the way people say "It is what it is." Some dumb phrase to patch up the emptiness. You just never know. God works in mysterious ways. He had a good life.

I shook my head, tried to knock something loose. "Since last year, since that break-in on Mallard where that old man died, I guess I've thought about being in spots like that, thought about what I'd do. In my mind, I always did the right thing. Before anyone else. Like someone on TV, you know? I always took the knife from the guy or chased down the kidnapper. Like there's this crash I hear while I'm getting the mail. And I go through the woods to the back of that house where that guy from the bank and his wife and all live. And there's people I can see through the back window. I picture myself going in, taking away their guns. Yelling things at them. Saving the kids. Doing whatever it takes."

"Yelling things?"

"Yeah. Like I play it all out. I'm going 'How many? How many?' Like yelling for the guy with the gun to tell me how many other bad guys are there. Then he looks up the stairs and I know there's someone behind me. And I spin around and put the dude's body in front of me and the other guy shoots him and I fire back and everyone's screaming and there I am, running through the house, yelling 'Clear' every time I get to an empty room."

"Jesus, Danny. There's something wrong with you."

I said I knew there was. I knew that I wasn't doing the thing, whatever it was. The thing I wanted to define me. I knew I was just hanging there, this tender flesh, a conveyer belt pulling me into the darkness.

"You've got to snap out of it."

I nodded, like it meant something, sitting there talking about nothing, her with me, so far away from the guy I thought I was.

"You alright?" she asked.

I nodded my head. Reflex. Then looked around. The metal rails in front of the cafeteria food, dull plastic trays being pushed along. "No," I said. "I'm pretty sure I'm not."

"That's okay," she said. "Nobody is."

The woman in blue scrubs was standing nearby, waiting for one of us to look up. She cleared her throat as Angie reached across the table for me.

The woman in blue scrubs coughed again. Her white sneakers making a sound against the linoleum floor, a high-pitched squeal, like someone far away opening the door in a house you thought was empty.

†

The DEBT

Hilary Davidson

A lonely hitchhiker was walking down the road on a sunny afternoon. All he carried with him was a knife inside his jacket pocket. He'd set out along this same stretch of highway before, too many times to count. Each step delivered a jolt of pain. If he stopped and untied his boots, he knew he'd feel relief for a split second, but that small freedom would be overshadowed by the agony of stuffing his blistered, bloody feet back in and continuing on. He had no choice. He had to go forward. A million steps. Ten million, maybe. A hundred million didn't seem out of the question. He couldn't count that high.

You should've stayed in school, you know.

The voice in his head sounded like his father. More accurately, it sounded like his father after the old man had downed a sufficient quantity of cheap whiskey, lying back in his La-Z-Boy, chain-smoking Camels and flipping channels.

Maybe if you'd stayed in school, you wouldn't be a bum. If you'd stayed in school, you wouldn't have turned into a lying, thieving mur ...

The hitchhiker tuned out the voice. That was his only luxury. It would be back, and it would bring friends, but on this sunny road, he didn't have to listen.

He felt the sun on his face, and he knew he should savor it. It was such a beautiful day, but it was spoiled by the dark knowledge of what he was going to do. He thought about a buddy of his. For the life of him, he couldn't remember the guy's name, but he had remnants of his Zen-and-pot-inspired aphorisms swirling around the edges of his mind. *Live in the moment. Stay right where you are. This moment is everything.*

There was laughter in his head, a whole choir splitting its sides. *You're living in the moment, all right.*

The hitchhiker heard a car behind him, and he half-turned to look. It was a silver Prius, of course. Always the silver Prius. It purred to a halt beside him.

"Hey, how you doing?" asked the driver. He was in his fifties, with a bad comb over and an eager expression on his fat face that suggested he wanted a pat on the head. "You need a ride?"

"Yeah," said the hitchhiker. He let a moment pass before opening the door. Then another. The driver's face didn't lose its puppy like enthusiasm.

What if I just run in the other direction? the hitchhiker thought. *What if I ....* But the question was already moot. His bloody foot-stumps were moving of their own volition, leading the rest of him into the vehicle.

"Sweet ride," he heard himself saying.

"Thanks. I got it because of the environment," said the older man. "I never used to care about stuff like that, thought the whole movement was for tree-hugging guys with squirrels for brains." He grinned at his own lame joke. "But my boy, he just went off to college. It's a whole different world now. Those climate-change deniers are crazy. Everything is getting worse. I keep thinking, what's the world going to be like when my boy gets older? What's it going to be like when he has kids of his own? Now I'm like this one-man reduce, reuse, recycle show."

The hitchhiker squirmed in his seat. A minute in this guy's presence, and he already felt stabby. Sure, change the world so your own kids and grandkids can go on enjoying it. Selfish bastard. It was all about him.

"You're about my son's age," the man said. "How do you feel about global warming?"

The hitchhiker had no feelings on the subject. For all he cared, the planet could heat itself up until it burst. Give the cockroaches a chance. But words flowed out of his mouth. He'd always been able to talk a good game. The first time he'd killed someone, he'd screwed up and got caught by the police. But he'd kept his composure, fronting innocence and throwing shade at another guy who he knew the cops would love to lock away. It wasn't a tough choice for them between a sweet-looking white boy with no priors, and a black kid who'd been busted for dope-dealing. It had worked out well for the hitchhiker in the end.

He ran his finger along the side of the big hunting knife inside his jacket. There were words inscribed on one side of the blade: *Numquam debitum retribui.*

"You want some water?" the driver asked. "There's a bottle by your feet."

Water. The mere mention of it made the hitchhiker weak with craving. He wanted it more than he'd wanted anything in his life. Even though he knew it was a trick, he fumbled for the bottle. His hands trembled as he opened it, and he thrust his head forward, hoping to catch a drop. Before he could, the bottle fell out of his hands, splashing water all over the floor of the Prius.

The driver didn't notice. "You in school, or taking some time for yourself?" His voice was amiable. "When I first went to college, I thought it wasn't for me, so I took some time off and went into the Peace Corps. I just felt called to serve, somehow. Afterwards, it was hard to go back. I traveled around for a while, then went back for my degree. I'm glad I did, even if it took me a hell of a long time."

The hitchhiker remembered that there was more to this conversation, but he was exhausted and only wanted for it to be over. He pulled the knife out of his jacket and leaned over, stabbing the man in the throat. Only instead of slumping over the wheel in a giant splurt of blood, the man stayed upright and kept talking.

"My boy's studying history. Most people don't see the point of that, but I believe in the value of a liberal arts education ..."

Another voice cut in from just behind the hitch-hiker's right ear. "You are not allowed to change a thing," it rasped. A pincer reached around to clasp his throat. Suddenly, the hitchhiker couldn't get air into his lungs, and even though he knew he was already dead, this terrified him.

"You play out the scene exactly as it happened in life. Over and over and over," the demon said. "One day, we may give you another of your victims to play with. But you will play out the crime in full each and every time."

The demon leaned closer, and the hitchhiker felt the creature's hot, wet breath against the back of his neck. It loosened its grip just enough to let him inhale its stench. His eyes filled with tears and he choked on bile in his throat.

"You are only in the first circle of Hell," it reminded him. "Things can get worse. Much worse."

The hitchhiker felt hundreds of burning needles digging into the back of his neck, and he made a weak squawking noise as the demon slurped and bit at him. The pain wasn't like anything he'd experienced in life. It vibrated through him, obliterating his mind and memory until there was nothing but agony.

"You're delicious," the demon said as it chewed. "Now, remember, numquam debitum retribui."

"The debt can never be repaid," gasped the hitchhiker through his sobs. Everything went dark around him. He could feel his body being pulled into a shadowy spiral. He'd never prayed in life, but now he prayed for oblivion.

When he opened his eyes, he was back where he started. A lonely hitchhiker, walking down the road on a sunny afternoon.

✝

The ZYGMA Gambit

Garnett Elliott

Kyler Knightly woke from a dream so lucid he knew it was prophetic. But he woke in the sleeping niche of his own room, not the Precog bays where he worked, and there were no electrodes attached to his temples or a somnograph humming away. He'd had the dream, the vision, under natural conditions.

Which meant it was very powerful.

Which meant it was coming true.

He rolled out of the niche, wondering how much time he had. "What time is it?" he asked the darkened room.

Ashurbanipal's richly cadenced voice, ever-present throughout Continuity Inc.'s headquarters, answered him. "That's a relative question, isn't it, Kyler?"

"I mean in the usual sense." The new AI had a quirky sense of humor.

"Per Greenwich Mean, it's 3:45 a.m., April 14th, 2223 A.D.—"

"Got it. Just turn the lights on, okay?"

"Another bout of insomnia, Kyler? You Dreamers are prone to that, you know."

"*Lights.*"

White glare spilled from a dozen concealed niches, illuminating Kyler's cramped living quarters. He muttered a curse. Sennacherib, the old AI, would've brought the lights on gradually, to the gentle strains of Bach or Liszt. But that was before the government had deregulated the Time Corps, before Continuity Inc. had snapped up the contract for policing past, present, and future. Happier days. Now a corporate mentality dominated.

He pulled on a pair of coveralls, followed by soft boots. "Coffee," he told the wall dispenser, which thankfully, did not have the capacity to talk back. A stream of black espresso squirted into a mug. Not Synthi-Caf or Neo Postum, but the real deal, grown and harvested beneath geodesic domes in Ecuador. Nothing but the best for employees charged with what was arguably the most important assignment in human history.

Protecting human history.

Kyler downed his expensive eye-opener and set off into the complex.

* * *

Constructed within lava tunnels of the Kerguelen Plateau, a micro-continent submerged beneath the Indian Ocean, Continuity Inc.'s headquarters sprawled over hundreds of square miles. Kyler took a shuttle from General Quarters to the Core, where the staging areas were set up. Even at this hour the complex buzzed with activity, as orange-smocked technicians hustled equipment through the honeycomb of hallways and chambers.

Ashurbanipal accosted him at the Core's first gate. "Kyler, what are you doing in this section? Your shift at the Precog bays is not due to begin until 8:00 a.m."

"I've got clearance."

"Yes, but your behavior is unusual. I might add: caffeine consumption at this stage during your sleep-cycle will likely disrupt productivity."

"Take it up with my supervisor."

"I will, Kyler. A Violet Level alert has already been sent to your personnel file."

"Noted. Now open the goddamn door."

The titanium valves of Gate One slid open. Invisible beams reached out to caress Kyler's body, assuring themselves of his unique biometrics. As a functioning pre-cog, he had enough value to the company to warrant advanced clearance. Anything less, and the short corridor he walked would be flooded with sarin in seconds.

Gate Two and Gate Three opened without further protest from Ashurbanipal. Kyler stepped out into Staging, his favorite part of the complex. A reinforced cavern the size of an aircraft hangar, the vast space echoed with the whine of multiple drills and auto-ratchets clanking as technicians tore down and put up sets.

He passed a mockup of Paddington Station circa 1884, featuring a Victorian era smoking car set on rails of authentic British Steel, ready to roar off into time and space. There was a cave from prehistoric France covered with soot-traced paintings (and littered with priceless flint artifacts), the shipboard cabin of Sir Francis Drake, an 'ultra-modern' living room from late 1950s North America, and the biggest set-piece of all, a marketplace of mud brick stalls and worked paving stones, dwarfed by the holographic image of a massive ziggurat, blazing in the artificial distance.

Kyler stalked by all these wonders, intent on a tarp-shrouded section marked with 'CLOSED SET' signs. The pieces he'd seen so far dealt only with the past, but he knew his uncle, Damon Cole, was assigned to a top-secret jaunt into the future.

He lifted a corner of tarp and ducked inside. The set appeared small when compared to the marketplace of Nineveh, but what it lacked in scale it made up in bizarreness: the holo backdrop depicted the landscape of Caliban Four, a moon of a white gas giant twenty light-years from Earth.

"Kyler!"

Damon had eased up out of a folding chair and was stepping toward him, moving with infinite caution in a pair of hip-high G-boots. For good reason: the boot's powerful servos, mimicking his thigh and calf muscles, would send him hurtling toward the cavern roof if he moved too fast. Watching him, Kyler felt the same flush of admiration he always did for his uncle, a top-rated Continuity operative. Dark-eyed and dark-bearded, he struck a physical contrast with Kyler's narrow build and high forehead. They shook hands like long-lost brothers.

"What are you doing here, Kyler? I'm supposed to jaunt in thirty minutes."

"That's just it. I had a dream ..."

His voice trailed off as he recalled the image: Damon, his legs shattered, lying sprawled on an alien world as an unseen presence came scuttling close.

"It's the boots," Kyler blurted, making a connection. "There's something wrong with them. Sabotage, maybe, I don't know. You're going to break your legs."

"What're you talking about? These boots were just checked out."

"It's going to happen. Dreams that clear never lie. You've got to abort, tell them you're sick or something."

Damon shook his head. "Can't do that, nephew. You know how important this jaunt is."

Kyler had been assigned precognitive duty with the Caliban Four project, and understood what was at stake. Continuity Inc. needed super-dense fissionables to power the Zygma Process, and the mining colony on the gas giant's moon had an abundant supply. Without such exotic fuels, all jaunts through time and space would cease. History would be vulnerable to any upstarts who had stumbled onto the secret of Zygma travel.

"No worries, Kyler." Damon clapped him on the shoulder. "You've warned me, so now I'll know to be extra careful."

His uncle's confidence failed to convince him. Unless he could do something, Damon would be jaunting off to his doom.

A glance around the set showed a pressurized suit and helmet, standing erect in a frame. Kyler recalled the CO_2 content of Caliban Four's atmosphere was too high for sustained breathing. An idea began to form.

"You got time for some coffee?" he asked Damon.

"Why not? I'm going to need to be alert, seeing as how I'll be impersonating a heavy-fuels buyer from five centuries in the future."

Damon sent a technician scurrying to fetch two fresh mugs. Kyler found a spot in one corner with crates stacked high, blocking casual view and any spy-beams from nosy Ashurbanipal. When the coffee came, they sat atop a holo-casing and sipped.

"You nervous?" Kyler asked, trying to conceal his own anxiety.

"Me? Nah. I've jaunted to the future before."

"What's the focus object?"

"An interesting little tidbit. I'll show it to you."

He left the corner, and his steaming mug. Kyler reached into his coveralls and took out four tablets of fast-dissolving Ultrazepam. One was usually enough to banish his insomnia. He slipped the little ovals into Damon's coffee just as his uncle was returning, wheeling over the pressure suit on a dolly.

"Take a look at this." He unclipped a chevron-shaped badge from the suit and tossed it to Kyler. A three-headed eagle had been sculpted onto the front.

"That," Damon said, "identifies me as a free trader from the Merchant House of Dorr, with a credit rating of up to one trillion Standard Monetary Units."

Kyler flipped the badge over. "I understand how Continuity Inc. gets their hands on focus objects from the past, but the future ...?"

"Don't think too hard about it," Damon said, reaching for his coffee. He sipped. If he tasted the Ultrazepam over the espresso, his face didn't show it. "Only Ashurbanipal has the brains to understand all this time-travel stuff."

Five minutes later he was slumping forward, his eyelids fluttering shut.

Kyler caught him and eased his unconscious body behind the holo-casing. He felt a twinge of guilt for tricking family, but told himself there was no other way. He pulled off the treacherous G-boots and slipped them on after a moment's hesitation. Somewhere inside the mechanics a short or a faulty lead must be waiting. He switched off the power; the boots became harmless pieces of metal attached to his legs.

"Hey, Damon," a voice called. "You're needed on the set."

Panicking, Kyler reached for the pressure suit and fumbled his way inside. The leggings fitted themselves neatly over the G-boots' bulk. He remembered to opaque the helmet before stepping out from behind the crates; a reasonable facsimile of Damon Cole. The suit's padding made up the difference in their physiques.

"Over here," a technician said, waving to a spot in the center of the stage. "Your mark's right there."

Kyler toed the neat X made by two pieces of tape. It occurred to him that he knew little of the jaunt's specifics, beyond Damon making some kind of deal for fuel. His heart began to thud against his ribs. Maybe he should've taken a tab of Ultrazepam for himself. He'd never jaunted before. As a Dreamer, his place was back at base, trying to peer into the future.

A Zygma projector poked toward him from among a bank of spotlights, its lens looking like a giant kaleidoscope pattern. He realized with a dull shock his job at Continuity Inc. was over. Finished. Even if he somehow managed to pull this mission off himself, management would never forgive him. Come to think of it, neither would Damon.

If he could pull this mission off.

"Alright, that's good," the technician said. "You okay in there, Damon? Ready?"

Kyler made the helmet nod.

"Great. *Lights.*"

The rest of the stage darkened, as two lamps on either side of the Zygma projector slid open. Twin beams stabbed out, to focus together on the identification badge attached to his chest.

"Bring up the intensity on the background a little more," the technician called. "Perfect. *Projector.*"

The kaleidoscope lens began to swirl, its snowflake patterns spiraling in on themselves. Kyler felt like he was being scrutinized by a diamond-eyed Cyclops. His stomach lurched.

"And ... *action!*"

The Zygma projector hummed and cracked. Invisible radiation streamed from the lens to pour over Kyler. Though no one but an AI could fully understand how the process worked, Kyler grasped the theory. The projector was forming a 'picture' of him and the background, with the badge as a focal point. At the same time, Zygma particles were subtracting every other element existing around him. The 'picture' became a puzzle-piece, with unique edges. In theory, this piece could only exist in two places: the Continuity Inc. set, and the actual time and space the set depicted.

But an object *can't* be in two places at once, so ...

Kyler shuddered, as the immutable laws of the Universe wrenched him from one reality and smoothed him into another. God's own fingertips seized the puzzle-piece and placed it where it would fit best.

The fourth moon of Caliban, 2750 A.D.

Kyler blacked out somewhere along the way.

* * *

An immense ball of white gas filled three-quarters of alien sky. Yellow, wispy clouds drifted, and on the horizon shone the double glare of a brilliant class F star and its red dwarf companion. Kyler squinted; even the opaque visor couldn't hold back the flood of light.

He forced himself to look down at the talc-fine powder beneath his feet. Caliban Four's heavy gravity seemed to reach up and grab him. While smaller than Earth, the gas giant's moon was several times denser. Kyler's one-hundred-fifty pound frame weighed two-twenty-five here. Not crushing, but his knees buckled with the added burden. He felt a sudden temptation to switch on the G-boots and squelched it. The damn things had started this whole mess.

Keeping his gaze from the dazzling sky, he looked around. About three hundred yards in the distance loomed a pyramid of black steel. The mining colony proper, he figured. Between it and him stretched a fenced walkway. Posts strung with shining wire—either charged or honed to molecular sharpness—separated the narrow path from the rest of the landscape, an endless vista of rolling hills. In the near-distance a forest of skeletal derricks jutted.

Simple enough. He started shuffling down the path. Moving under 1.5 G's felt like wading through waist-deep water. Ten steps and he was already winded. The steel pyramid seemed to recede another hundred yards. He felt truly sorry he hadn't ditched his G-boots; the inert metal clinging to his legs slowed him further.

And what are you going to say when you get inside? Please hand me over half a ton of Palladium 23? He wasn't a natural diplomat like his uncle Damon. Hell, he got tongue-tied talking to girls.

He recalled one important fact: Continuity Inc. had sent an agent here already, about a week prior to Damon's scheduled jaunt. Recon mission or some such. With luck, he might still be around. The agent's name was Huxley, and there was something unusual about his appearance ... Kyler didn't remember what, exactly.

A sign attached to one of the fence posts halted his thoughts. The strange Anglic characters took a moment for his helmet-visor to translate.

WARNING! FENCE COMPROMISED NEXT 100 YARDS. BEWARE VELOCIPEDES.

The visor's translation neglected to explain what a 'velocipede' was. But sure enough, the wires ahead had been snapped in places and lay in glossy snarls. He patted at the side pockets of his pressure suit. No weapons. And why would a free trader on a peaceful mission of commerce need any?

He took a tentative step forward. White sand rose in a little puff from a nearby hill. Movement? Or maybe it was just wind. He continued his shuffling pace from before. About thirty yards down the walkway several more white puffs appeared, closer.

He tried to break into a run. It felt more like a spirited walk. The approaching puffs became a miniature sand storm. He heard a rumbling sound at first, but moments later it grew more distinct. Scuttling. The same noise he'd heard in his dream. Low-slung shapes appeared within the whirling powder.

He'd never reach the steel pyramid before those creatures. Instinct made him veer off the path through a section of sundered wire. The shadows of the tall mining derricks fell across him. He'd make for those; it might be possible to climb the lattice of beams to safety.

A glance over his shoulder brought a horrifying sight. The dust was being churned by hundreds of pairs of bowed legs, attached to the slick gray carapaces of ten-foot centipedes. They came swirling after him, legs undulating like the ranks of oars on an Old Earth trireme. Mandibles the size of pruning shears flashed open and closed. The pack was less than fifty yards away, and gaining.

He wouldn't make the derrick. Not at this pace. Only the G-boots could give him a fighting chance—if they didn't shatter his legs. He reached for the power switch at his waist. Hesitated.

The velocipedes were at thirty yards. Close enough that he could see the clockwork of their smaller mouthparts, meshing together in anticipation.

"Get down" called a gruff voice.

Near the base of the closest derrick a woman was waving at him. 'Woman' being a guess; she had a bull-neck and squat, blocky body. Instead of a pressure suit she wore reflective coveralls.

"I said *down.*"

She'd unslung some type of rifle. Kyler let himself stumble midstride and hit the sand. Heavy gravity made the impact hurt more than it should have. He heard a sharp *snap* and felt something molten pass over his back. Keeping flat, he scrabbled around to get a look. Several more *snaps*, several bolts of crimson plasma, and the velocipedes were reduced to swirling ash.

The woman jumped down from the derrick and waddled over. "You alright?"

"Nothing broken." Kyler got to his feet.

"They were gonna kill you. You saw that, right? You'd vouch for that?"

She wore a pair of bubble-shaped goggles over her eyes, and a tiny respirator covering her nose and mouth. But for that and the reflective clothing, her burnt-bronze skin was exposed to the elements of Caliban Four. "There's a fine," she said, "for every velocipede you kill. It's in the charter. Part of that bullshit 'Indigene

Protection Act.' But it's justified, if they're fixing to kill *you*."

The voder clipped to Kyler's ear translated her Anglic speech, right down to the accent. And it translated his words back. "Thanks. I'll make whatever kind of statement you need."

"What're you doing out here, anyway?"

"I'm, ah, a free trader from House Dorr ..."

"Where the hell's your ship?" She looked up first at the sky, then the surrounding hills. "Or your landing boat?"

"I was dropped off."

Beneath the goggles, her eyes narrowed. "Alright. Be mysterious, even though I just saved your life." She held out a thick hand. "Name's Emma."

"Kyler." He couldn't think of anything else. Her grip felt like a hydraulic press.

"If you're the free trader everyone's been talking about, the CFO will want to meet you, stat."

He looked glumly at the black pyramid, still a ways off. "Don't tell me you hoofed it here."

"Nah, nah. Not with dangerous indigenes about." She waved toward a six-wheeled buggy parked just behind the derrick. "We'll take you back on that."

Kyler's heart lifted at the prospect of motorized transport. Emma closed a panel at the derrick's base, picked up a toolbox, and shuffled toward the buggy. More tools jangled from her belt. Walking behind her, Kyler eyed the still-hot barrel of the plasma rifle nestled between her shoulder blades. Back in 2223 A.D., the technology to accelerate plasma would require at least five feet of magnetic coils.

"I noticed you had trouble running," she said, when they reached the vehicle. "Something wrong with your exo?"

She meant the G-boots. "Yeah, a short, I think. I've been afraid to turn it on."

"I'll take a look when we get back. Real uncomfortable, a skinny-legger like you trying to move around without one."

"I appreciate that. You've been more than helpful."

"Us frontier types usually are." She started the buggy's engine. "Give my boss a fair price on that fuel, and we'll call it even."

* * *

The "boss" of Caliban Extraction and Refining, Ltd., turned out to be Hyram Gose, an older man built like Emma, but with a near-spherical belly and legs thick as tree trunks. He wore a black cape to distinguish himself from the rest of the mining stiffs. They were *all* built like Emma, adapted to the gravity of Caliban's fourth moon by aggressive gene engineering. Kyler felt self-conscious of his narrow limbs when he removed the pressure suit.

"So you're the buyer from House Dorr, eh?" Hyram said, after he and Kyler had retired to a private office, lit on three sides by holo-displays of a lush, forested landscape. "It's a little strange they sent someone out here directly, instead of dickering over a commo laser."

Kyler tried to answer, but found his voice gasping.

"Something wrong?"

"The air's a little thin."

Hyram nodded, none too concerned. "The pressure's several millibars less than what you're used to. We'll prepare quarters in the off-worlder's section of the complex."

"Quarters? I thought we'd negotiate the deal now."

Hyram's bass laughter seemed to echo through the surrounding forest. "Just like a merchant. Right to business, eh? Well, it's not that simple. I have to get a market report, then confer with the proxy AI's for the board of directors … it'll take a day or so. That quick enough?"

"No hurry," Kyler lied.

"Good. In the meantime, I'll have Emma show you around. Give you the nickel tour of the place. Just keep in mind, a frontier mining colony's not the same as a trading floor. Things can get rough. One of these guys throws a punch, it's likely to snap your neck."

"Noted," Kyler said, and gulped air.

* * *

Caliban Extraction and Refining boasted only one bar, but the lounge attached was cavernous, paneled in dozens of different metals, from burnished gallium to soft gold, with slightly-oxidized iron predominating. Emma found a secluded table and hustled over two beers in copper steins. Kyler took a grateful sip; rich-tasting ale, full of hops. He guzzled, averting his eyes from the floor show some twenty feet away. A pair of

Caliban natives, male and female, removed their clothing to heavily syncopated music.

"You some kind of prude?" Emma asked.

"Ah, no, it's just that ..."

"We think you off-worlders are pretty ugly, too." She smiled when she said it. "Let me ask you another question: you got any enemies, back at that merchant establishment you're from?"

"What do you mean?"

"I had a look at your exo-legs. Aside from the fact the servos are Stone Age primitive, someone rigged them to overload as soon as the battery draw went to ten mega-amps. Which, coincidentally, is the power requirement for walking around on Caliban Four."

"You're talking sabotage."

"Exactly."

Kyler hid his reaction behind a long pull of ale.

"Other interesting thing," Emma went on. "Two days before you arrived, a bunch of automated tractors went nuts and plowed through the southern section of monowire fence. Near where I found you. We had enough time to put up a sign, but not fix anything."

"That ever happen before?"

"Never. C.E.R.'s got the highest safety rating in this system."

"So you're saying ..."

"Someone's trying to kill you."

Or Damon Cole, Kyler thought. He drained his stein and set it down with a clank. "Have you heard of a man named Huxley? He'd be an off-worlder like me, a newcomer."

"The surveyor?" Emma rolled her eyes. "He showed up about a week ago. Wants to map out the northern pole caverns, 'stead of just letting the probes do it."

"Why'd you make that face?"

"I don't have nothing against cyborgs, personally, but he could be a little more subtle about his appearance, you know what I mean?"

Kyler recalled that Huxley had suffered a terrible injury during a jaunt to the Middle Ages. The Continuity physicians had done what they could. "You know where I can find him?"

Emma's mouth twitched at the corners. "How do you know Huxley? It's a big galaxy, mister. I'm beginning to—"

An open palm smacked against the table, startling both of them. Kyler hadn't heard the big miner-type's approach over the music. His coveralls were unbuttoned to the waist, revealing a large 'V' of hirsute muscle. Chrome beads hung from his mustachios.

"You partial to skinny guys now, Emma?" The man waved thick knuckles at Kyler.

"Oh, hell, Kal. I didn't know you were the jealous kind."

"As soon as a new swingin' dick hits the planet, you're all over it."

Kyler started to say something conciliatory, but Emma's chair was already scraping back. She stood and faced the man. Without warning, her booted foot shot forward and struck him in the shin. He bent, his dark skin flushing darker. As he straightened, he swung out with the back of his fist, catching Emma across the nose. She staggered back.

Maybe it was the beer, or the general lack of oxygen feeding his brain, but Kyler got up so quickly bright stars trailed at the corners of his eyes. He grabbed his empty stein and slammed it against Kal's head. The metal cylinder flattened on impact, though Kal didn't do more than grunt. He kept his attention fixed on Emma as she regained her balance.

Kyler snatched up a metal chair and hauled it over his head. He groaned with effort; the chair weighed more than it should, and there was a shooting pain in his back like he'd pulled something. But he managed to bring it down across Kal's shoulders. Shock traveled through the metal and stung his wrists. For his part, Kal grunted louder this time, and turned to face the panting off-worlder. His eyes showed a mixture of amusement and menace.

"You got a gun or a knife, son?" he asked. "'Cause otherwise, you're not—"

Emma's punch cut him off. She landed a short one to Kal's ribs, stepped back, and threw a hook to the groin. Kal's eyes crossed. He tottered in a little circle before sitting down, hard, on a nearby stool.

"Serves you right, you goddamn bull moose," she said. "This fella I'm entertaining here is going to close a big deal with the company."

"I think you cracked his ribs," Kyler said.

"Nothing that won't heal in a day or two. Ain't that right, Kal?"

"Sure thing, honey. And that was a nice combination, there."

"Kal's my husband," Emma said. "He's the insecure type, on account of his substandard pecker. Though in truth, I'd kick his ass if he didn't start a fight over me once in a while."

"Just showing I care."

"Damn straight." Emma slapped Kal's broad shoulder. "And you, Kyler, you hadn't stepped in like you're supposed to, I'd be kicking your ass right now, too. I did save your life, after all."

"Absolutely."

She planted her hands on her broad hips and gave a satisfied nod. "That's what I like to see. Two level-headed males who know their place. Now let's all have us another round."

* * *

Still reeling from Caliban ale, Kyler followed Emma back to her shop and tried on the newly repaired G-boots. Several careful paces convinced him they were no longer treacherous. He begged off the rest of the tour and set out on his own, looking for Huxley among the cramped metal corridors of the C.E.R. pyramid. Even with the boots' assistance he had to stop periodically and catch his breath.

After an hour he found him, bent over a surface rover in one of the vehicle bays. Even without the brushed titanium covering one side of his head he stood out; tall and long-limbed, like Kyler, and wearing a full-body exoskeleton for convenience. He was fiddling with the rover's engine, holding a live fusion welder in his left hand.

Kyler cleared his throat. When the cyborg didn't look up, he said: "Huxley?"

A half-fleshed face turned to his. Huxley's left eye was a ruby-iris lens, humming as it twisted into focus. "Who're you?"

"I'm from Continuity. The heavy fuels mission—"

"Keep your voice down." Huxley switched off his voder and motioned for Kyler to do the same. "You're not Damon Cole."

"I was a last minute replacement."

The ruby lens swept over Kyler from head to toe. "You're Kyler Knightly, Level Two Dreamer. You haven't been cleared for field work."

"There was an emergency. They had no choice but to send me in."

"Not likely." The flesh part of Huxley's face frowned. "The mission's scrubbed."

"It's still viable. I've got a meeting scheduled with Hyram Gose to negotiate the buy."

Huxley set the welder down. The normal part of his face seemed to lose concentration, and when he spoke his voice had a flat, metallic edge. "The mission's been compromised. Activate your recall beacon, now."

"Can't do that. We've spent too much time preparing for this jaunt, and I've already introduced myself to the C.E.R. staff. If I leave now, without the fuel, Continuity might not be able to jaunt again."

Another pause. Kyler could've sworn the processors from Huxley's mechanical side were debating with his brain cells. No wonder Emma had been unnerved.

"I'm ranking officer," Huxley said at last. "I recommend we scrub the mission."

"Huh-uh." No matter what trouble waited when he got back, Kyler owed his uncle to at least try.

"I see you're committed."

"Aren't you going to help me? That's why they sent you here, isn't it?"

"I was tasked to aid Damon Cole, covertly. You're not Damon Cole."

Kyler nodded toward the rover. "What the hell are you doing, anyway?"

"Maintaining my cover."

"And what good is that if the mission's already compromised?"

"Likely, Continuity will send another, more competent, operative."

Kyler took a step backward. "Great. I'll be sure to let management know what a stand-up guy you are."

The ruby-iris watched impassively as Kyler left the bay.

* * *

The off-worlder's "suite" was a ten by ten cubicle, but it could be pressurized to Earth-standard, and had a tub in one corner. Once submerged in warm water, Kyler's body felt freed from the shackles of extra weight. That, and the convenience of breathing easily, gave him an opportunity to think.

Someone had sabotaged Damon's G-boots prior to the jaunt. Someone had also sabotaged the fences surrounding the area where Damon was likely to appear. Anyone from Continuity could've done the former; only one person here would have had the advance knowledge for the latter.

The vents to his room hissed as the pressurization cycled on again. He considered several ways of confronting Huxley, and dismissed them all. Too risky. He needed to complete the buy and get out of here as quickly as possible. His recall beacon housed one of a pair of entangled quantum particles; activating it would send a signal down the timestream. Zygma energy could bring him back to 2223 A.D. within minutes— hopefully with heavy fissionables clenched in his hands.

He felt a headache starting. The pressure vents should've shut off by now, but they were still blowing strong. He got out of the tub, dripping, and went over to adjust the environmental controls. They didn't respond.

Annoyed, he hit the intercom button to report the problem. It too, failed to respond.

The hiss of incoming air became a roar.

He had a sinking feeling about the door, but he tried it anyway. Frozen shut. Now it felt like someone was squeezing his head in a vice. He could only take shuddering breaths.

His G-boots lay atop the narrow bed. He struggled into them, snapping shut the catches around his naked thighs and calves. With the power at one hundred percent, he strode toward the door and kicked with his heel. The metal shook, but didn't give.

He doubled the power draw. Servos whined protest as he kicked again. The door dented in the middle. Still intact.

Blackness came crowding at the edge of his vision. The two kicks had left him starved for oxygen, but taking a full breath in high pressure could burst his lungs. He swayed; the little room spun. Enough time for one more try.

He trebled the power.

Fat blue sparks leapt from the boots' muscle-strands. There was a screeching sound as the desperate kick burst a seam along one edge of the door, followed by a whoosh as air rushed out into the hallway.

Slowly, the pressure equalized. Blackness fled from Kyler's temples. When he could breathe again, he called out through the seam for help. Minutes later, several voices echoed from the hall. The door wrenched back. Hyram Gose stood just outside, his eyes puffy with sleep.

"What the hell happened?"

"Someone messed with the pressure controls for my room." *And I have good idea who it was.*

Hyram grimaced. "Emma said something funny was going on."

"Look, whoever's doing this really doesn't want our business deal to happen. Can we just speed things up, make the buy, so I can get out of here safely?"

Hyram stroked his chin. "This could all be some elaborate scam, to get me to lower the price …"

"By risking my life?"

"You *are* a trader, after all."

"How about this: I won't wheedle you. I'll pay a flat fee, plus an expediting bonus."

That seemed to convince him. "Get dressed and I'll meet you in the boardroom in ten minutes. I'll leave a guard outside."

* * *

Ten minutes later, his hair combed and wearing the House Dorr badge clipped to his chest, Kyler sat down at an imitation rosewood table in a large room. One of the walls sloped at a forty-five degree angle. Made of transparent densiplast, it permitted a panoramic view of the ever-blazing landscape.

Across from Kyler sat Hyram Gose, Emma, and four flickering holo-busts of distinguished people.

"Proxy AIs," Hyram explained, lighting a fat cigar. "They represent C.E.R.'s Board of Directors. Personality constructs, accurate down to the eye-twitch. Can't make a move without 'em."

The busts nodded in unison, stiffly.

Kyler cleared his throat. "I'm a little unclear of the protocols out here on the frontier. Where I'm from it's customary for you to make the opening offer."

Hyram glanced at Emma. "Alright." He puffed while he entered a number onto a data-slate, then slid the device across the table.

Kyler blinked. The figure exceeded his one trillion credit rating. "It seems a little steep."

"Emma," Hyram said, "bring in the fuel. I want to show our friend here what he's bargaining for."

Emma left and returned moments later holding an object that looked like a lunch box. She set it down on the table with a heavy thump.

Hyram pointed the cigar. "At total-conversion rates, there's enough refined Palladium 23 in there to power a core world for a year."

Or a Zygma projector for the foreseeable future. "Impressive." Not knowing what else to do, Kyler entered a counter-proposal exactly half of Hyram's figure and slid it over.

"What's this? I thought you said you wouldn't wheedle. And where's the expediting bonus?"

They went back and forth like that until sweat began to drip from Kyler's brow. Hyram's face was stone-like, unreadable as he conferred in whispers with the chorus of AIs. Emma only frowned. After an interminable period, Hyram shocked Kyler by agreeing at a price seventy-five percent of his maximum credit rating.

"You do your House proud," the CFO said at last.

Emma's face cracked into a smile. Kyler got the impression he'd been taken, but not outright fleeced. "The fuel's mine?"

"We'll send you the bill."

He reached across the table and pulled the container of Palladium 23 close. Tugging a boulder would've been easier. But here it was: the future of Continuity Inc., and hopefully, his ticket out of the brig when he returned. He made cheerful small-talk with Hyram while his left hand crept down and activated the recall beacon hidden in his belt.

"What're your plans now?" Emma asked.

"I'll be leaving soon," he said, truthfully. He wondered how the pair would react minutes from now, when Zygma particles suddenly subtracted him from their reality.

A startled cry echoed just outside the boardroom. The door slammed inward, shouldered by Huxley. His exo-skeleton whirred with barely-restrained power as he stalked into the room, brandishing a sparking fusion cutter like a sword.

The half-real face swiveled toward Kyler. When Huxley spoke, the calm, measured voice wasn't his own. "You've forced my hand."

Ashurbanipal's voice.

"Security!" Hyram bellowed, and launched himself in a flying tackle. The cutter flashed. Hyram Gose flopped apart in two cauterized pieces, separated at the torso. His black cape fluttered to the ground.

Heedless, Emma charged in from the flank, fists raised. Huxley caught her with an exo-boosted open hand. She flew across the table and struck imitation paneling, her head making a squat indentation in the wood.

"You weren't supposed to be here," said Ashurbanipal/Huxley. He closed the distance to Kyler's chair in two rapid strides. Up came the cutter for a downward swing.

In his mind's eye Kyler saw it: the exact arc the fusion blade would travel. Precognition? He'd never had a vision while conscious before. But as the cutter descended, he knew where to leap aside. His own exo-legs gave him a burst of speed. The blade sliced his chair in half and sunk deep into the floor.

Huxley uttered a very human grunt. He had difficulty pulling the cutter free. Kyler glanced past him to where Emma lay sprawled, her scalp cut and flowing, possibly dead. The image filled him with murderous resolve. He kicked out, the ball of his foot striking Huxley mid-thigh. Titanium rods protected the muscle, but the blow's force sent Huxley reeling backward into the table. He dropped his cutter. Without hesitation, Kyler scooped it up and thrust. The blade sheared through Huxley's ruby-iris lens in a shower of sparks, the bright tip protruding from the top of his metal-plated head. The cyborg's human lips contorted; his eye rolled back as he shook with uncontrollable spasms.

Kyler dropped the cutter. He rushed to Emma and felt her wrist for a pulse. Strong. Her eyelids were already beginning to flicker open. High gravity made for thick skulls. He spared a glance at Hyram's smoking remains; not even ultra-tech medicine could repair *that*.

Not much time left. He hurried around the table to where the container of Palladium 23 sat. It had to be in his hands when he traveled back, otherwise the trip had been for nothing.

Out in the hallway a klaxon sounded.

"He—he wanted an upgrade," Huxley said, his teeth chattering.

By reflex, Kyler reached for the cutter. But Huxley was no longer a threat. He lay sprawled across the table, breathing in wracking convulsions. The wounded side of his head fizzled and sparked.

"What did you say?"

"Ashurbanipal ... downloaded part of himself, into me. Took over. He wanted ROM chips from the future to upgrade himself." Huxley craned his head around to nod toward the proxy AIs, watching them with appalled looks on their digitized faces.

"Why did he try to kill Damon?"

"So that—" Huxley shook all over. He bit into his lower lip, drawing blood.

"Never mind that. Where's your recall beacon?"

The cyborg made a faint gesture toward his belt. Kyler reached over, found the switch and activated it.

From the hallway came the tromping of boots. Long-barreled plasma rifles poked through the shattered door. Kyler saw a face peek in and blanch when it caught sight of Hyram.

The air shimmered with blue-white motes. Time did an awkward stop-start, the security guards freezing for a moment, then spilling through the doorway. Freezing again.

The backdrop of Caliban Four dissolved into cosmic static.

* * *

He did not lose consciousness during the jaunt back. Instead, he watched as the swirling motes reassembled themselves into a familiar tarp-shrouded set, complete with Zygma projectors, lights, and orange-garbed technicians. Damon stood with arms folded, his jaw set so firm the tendons on his neck bulged. Flanking him were two Continuity agents in black uniforms. Both had their sidearms drawn and pointing toward Kyler.

Uh-oh. He looked down to see the container of Palladium 23 clenched between both hands. There was that, at least.

"You're under arrest," Damon said.

Ashurbanipal's voice broke in: "I recommend summary execution, as per the Continuity Inc. bylaws, section 6C. 'No personnel may interfere with a mission identified as Top Priority, under penalty of—"

"Noted," Damon said.

"Hold on a second." Kyler set the fuel down, slow, so as not to excite any trigger-fingers. His voice shaking, he narrated the events of his jaunt to Caliban Four, including Huxley's damning testimony.

"You got any proof of this?" Damon asked. His tendons weren't bulging as much.

"Any minute now, when Huxley shows up. He might be dead, but you can still check his processors for Ashurbanipal's influence."

The overhead lights turned red. "I'm instituting a Code One Alert," Ashurbanipal announced. "All personnel to enter lockdown."

"Override!" Damon yelled. "Priority omega aught delta. AI functions cease."

The lights flickered back to normal. Ashurbanipal droned protest, but his voice died away.

"Do you believe me now, uncle?" Kyler asked.

Damon nodded, his lips curled in disgust. "The old AI, Sennacherib, pulled something similar. We hard-wire them so they *can't* improve their intelligence, but they always try …"

"What would be the point in killing you? Why not just have Huxley return once he'd stolen the ROM chips?"

"That's simple enough. Without fuel, Continuity can't make any more jaunts. So no one can go back in time and try to undo Ashurbanipal's work."

"We'll have to wipe his core."

"Yeah, I'm afraid so. Maybe 'Hammurabi' or 'Nebuchadnezzar' will be different." Damon gave the container of Palladium 23 a playful kick. "Good work, that. For someone without formal field training or experience, you did well on your first jaunt."

Kyler thought of Emma. "I had some help."

"Well, after we sort all this mess out with the brass, I'll put you in for a promotion. Who knows? Maybe you and me could partner on a jaunt."

"I'd like that, Uncle Damon. I'd like that very much."

†

ABOUT THE AUTHORS

PATTI ABBOTT is the author of more than 100 stories online, in print, and in numerous anthologies. Recent stories appeared in *The Huffington Post, Kwik Krimes, Reloaded, Pulp Modern,* and *Plots with Guns.* Forthcoming stories will appear in *Needle: A Magazine of Noir, Thuglit, Crimespree Magazine, Malfeasance Occasional,* and *Underground Voices Anthology.* She is the author of two ebooks, *Home Invasion* and *Monkey Justice.*

EVAN VLADIMIR CORDER spends his time analyzing philosophical arguments, constructing anagrams, and mentally climbing Penrose stairs. He lives for good dream recall and writing dark fiction.

HILARY DAVIDSON won the 2011 Anthony Award for Best First Novel for *The Damage Done.* That book launched a series that continued with *The Next One to Fall*—set in Peru—and *Evil In All Its Disguises,* about a missing journalist in Acapulco. Hilary's first standalone novel, *Blood Always Tells,* is published by Forge. She's also the author of a short story collection, *The Black Widow Club.* Her first tale for BEAT to a PULP, "Insatiable," won a Spinetingler Award, and her contribution to *BEAT to a PULP: Round Two,* "A Special Kind of Hell," was a finalist for a Derringer.

GARNETT ELLIOTT lives and works in Tucson, Arizona. He's had stories appear in *Alfred Hitchcock's Mystery Magazine*, *Needle: A Magazine of Noir*, *Reloaded (Both Barrels 2)*, *Uncle B's Drive-In Fiction*, *Blood and Tacos*, *Battling Boxing Stories*, and numerous online magazines and print anthologies.

CHRIS F. HOLM was born in Syracuse, New York, the grandson of a cop who passed along his passion for crime fiction. His work has appeared in such publications as *Ellery Queen's Mystery Magazine*, *Alfred Hitchcock's Mystery Magazine*, *Needle: A Magazine of Noir*, and *The Best American Mystery Stories 2011*. He's been an Anthony Award nominee, a Derringer Award finalist, and a Spinetingler Award winner. His "Collector" novels, published by Angry Robot books, recast the battle between heaven and hell as Golden Era crime pulp.

Twice short-listed for Best American Mystery Stories, TERRIE FARLEY MORAN's cozy mystery novel *Well Read, Then Dead* is the first book in the "Read 'Em and Eat Café and Bookstore" series. Terrie tells anyone willing to listen that hanging out with any or all of her seven grandchildren provides life's grand and joyful moments.

STEVE WEDDLE grew up on the Louisiana/Arkansas line, holds an MFA in creative writing from Louisiana State University, and currently works for a newspaper group. His debut novel, *County Hardball*, is published by Tyrus Books. His fiction is represented by Stacia Decker of the Donald Maass Literary Agency. He lives with his family in Virginia.

A poem by Kyle J. Knapp from
   Celebrations in the Ossuary ...

THE PERFECT DAY

Give me just a day
   Of homemade wine,
Spray-painted sunflowers,
19th century prose,
Sordid, puerile jokes,
Dried maple leaves to crush in our palms
A pale too-old sun to dance beyond

And her laughter—

**The debut
poetry collection,
*Pluvial Gardens***

 BEAT to a PULP
PO Box 173
Freeville, New York 13068
USA
Email: btapzine@beattoapulp.com
Visit us at www.beattoapulp.com